PUSSYFOOTIN' PREY

"What is it that you hunt, Gunn? Men? Women?" Betsy was pumping Gunn for information, but she wasn't getting very far.

I hunt meat, when I have to." Gunn responded, knowing Betsy was after something, but not able to figure out what. At any rate, she made him very uncomfortable — something few women could do.

Betsy rose from her chair and walked slowly to where Gunn was seated. Her breasts were at eye level. Gunn looked up — into Betsy's eyes. He saw something cunning in the way they gleamed.

"What ever it is you want, Betsy, I can't help you unless you stop pussyfootin' around."

"You know what I want, Gunn," she said. Her voice was husky in her throat. Then she leaned forward and gave him a long, lingering kiss.

Whatever Betsy was trying to find out, she must have wanted it pretty bad. So Gunn decided to give her a big hint!

MORE EXCITING WESTERNS FROM ZEBRA!

THE GUNN SERIES BY JORY SHERMAN

GUNN #12: THE WIDOW-MAKER   (987, $2.25)
Gunn offers to help the lovely ladies of Luna Creek when
the ruthless Widow-maker gang kills off their husbands.
It's hard work, but the rewards are mounting!

GUNN #13: ARIZONA HARDCASE   (1039, $2.25)
When a crafty outlaw threatens the lives of some lovely
females, Gunn's temper gets mean and hot—and he's got
no choice but to shoot it off!

GUNN #14: THE BUFF RUNNERS   (1093, $2.25)
Gunn runs into two hell-raising sisters caught in the middle
of a buffalo hunter's feud. He hires out his sharpshooting
skills—and doubles their fun!

THE BOLT SERIES BY CORT MARTIN

BOLT #6: TOMBSTONE HONEYPOT   (1009, $2.25)
In Tombstone, Bolt meets up with luscious Honey
Carberry who tricks him into her beehive. But Bolt has a
stinger of his own!

BOLT #7: RAWHIDE WOMAN   (1057, $2.25)
Rawhide Kate's on the lookout for the man who killed her
family. And when Bolt snatches the opportunity to come to
Kate's rescue, she learns how to handle a tricky gun!

BOLT #8: HARD IN THE SADDLE   (1095, $2.25)
When masked men clean him of his cash, Bolt's left in a
tight spot with a luscious lady. He pursues the gang—and
enjoys a long, hard ride on the way!

#14

THE BUFF RUNNERS

GUNN

BY JORY SHERMAN

ZEBRA BOOKS
KENSINGTON PUBLISHING CORP.

Dedication

This one's in memory of Ken Rothrock—a hell of a writer, a hell of a friend. He knew the country. He was here. May he rest easy.

ZEBRA BOOKS

are published by

KENSINGTON PUBLISHING CORP.
475 Park Avenue South
New York, N.Y. 10016

CHAPTER ONE

There was something bad in the air that day in San Antonio.

A bad taste to the air.

A stench to it.

A twisted feeling that something was wrong.

Gunn felt it the minute he and Jed Randall rode into town, saw a man stagger from one saloon and into another, heard the loud laughter from each.

"They start a mite early," said Jed Randall, a friend who sometimes rode with Gunn.

It was a little after nine in the morning.

Horses lined the street, buckboards, a sulky, some spring wagons, some mules. Yet it wasn't a Saturday, and this wasn't the busiest part of town. The livery stable was halfway down the street and the two men had to thread their way through a lot of foot traffic to get there. Men walked back and forth who looked as if they belonged to the age of the forty-niners or who would look more at home attending a mountain man rendezvous back in '37. They ambled back and forth, tipping bottles up, talking loudly, staggering. The Red Dog Saloon belched two men out in the street, who appeared to have been tossed there by a kicking mule. They didn't move after their bodies thudded into the street. Across the street, the Wild Cat seemed to be packed with more rowdies than you could see at a dogfight, and the men inside seemed even louder than those in the Red Dog.

And a few men taking a breather outside, took time

to throw some dirty looks at Gunn and Randall. Just for good measure.

"Sure you want to bed down here, Jed? Seems to me you could take a bath in the San Antone River and get just as clean."

"Hell, we're here now. Wonder what's goin' on?"

"I'd consider giving some thought before asking."

"Yeah."

The man inside the livery wasn't in a good mood, either.

He looked up from his steaming shovel, cocked an eyebrow as the two men dismounted, stepped inside, leading their horses.

"Everything's two dollars," he grumbled.

"Stalls, a place to hang the saddles, grain, water," said Gunn.

"Two dollars each. Good dollars. Greenbacks. No bank notes. Spanish or Yocum silver. Gold."

"Might particular, ain't you?" asked Jed.

"I got my hands full, mister. You find a stall, pay me and do your own feeding and currying."

Gunn fished out a wad of bills from his denims, unwrapped four singles. He stuffed them in the liveryman's shirt pocket. The man walked to the end of the barn, threw the green horseapples out the back. They splatted in a puddle of brown water. The man added a stream of tobacco juice to the ground.

"Last two stalls are yonder," he said, waving the shovel on the opposite side of the huge barn. Hang your tack on the back wall, tag 'em those numbered buttons. Grain barrel's over in the corner. Haul your own water."

Jed said something under his breath.

Gunn led his horse, Esquire, to the stall, stripped him down, backed him in, removed the bridle. Ten minutes later, they were finished.

6

"Place to stay close by?" he asked the liveryman.

"On Juniper Street? This ain't where the cattlemen go. Bunch of godamned stinking buff runners."

"Any place will do," said Gunn quietly, wondering what the man was babbling about. "We aren't staying long."

"Hell, makes me no never mind. They's a flop house down the street. The Nueces. Can't miss it. It's the one smells of raw meat been out in the sun too long."

Gunn narrowed his pale blue eyes. He was a tall man, wide-shouldered, tanned face, lean features, sensuous lips. His dark hair was shaggy, long, reaching almost to his shoulders. He wore a kerchief around his neck, a leather vest hanging on his big frame, a Colt .44 strapped to his hip, a Mexican knife slim in its scabbard.

"We could bed down here, Jed," he said. "Might be cleaner."

Randall laughed drily. He had come to know Gunn's humor after riding a trail or two with him. Jed was a half a foot shy of six feet, with straw hair, laugh wrinkles at the corners of his brown eyes. He walked with the bowed legs of a man who had spent as much time in the saddle as on the ground. He was a slow-burner, more interested in working cattle than bunkhouse brawls, but when pushed he was no lily-livered wallflower. If the ball was opened, Jed would dance. The two men had just delivered a herd of prime Mexican beef to the Quartermaster Depot at the Post of San Antonio. They were building a new fort there on land donated by the city. The drive from Laredo had taken half a month or more and the two men were about ten pounds heavier with the dust they packed.

"You got a trough we could use?" said Randall, going along with the joke.

The liveryman frowned, tugged at his right ear.

"You boys go on some'eres else and have your fun. I got horseshit to shovel."

Gunn and Jed laughed, walked from the livery, lugging saddle bags and bedrolls, Winchesters that had long since lost their bluing. They passed between the two saloons, saw the hotel down the street. A buggy suddenly swerved in their path as a man on wobbly legs reached up and snared the reins. A small bunch of roughnecks lounged on the boardwalk, laughing at this bit of tomfoolery.

As the buggy swerved, Gunn saw that it was driven by a young pretty woman with dark brown hair wearing a calico dress. she tried to jerk the reins out of the man's hand, her face dark with a scowl. She wore no bonnet and her hair glistened coppery bright in the sun.

The man was drunk. He staggered, wobbled, but held on to the reins. He jerked the horse up short, backed it up.

"Go on, Elmer, give Betsy what-for!" yelled one of the youths sitting on the boardwalk.

"Yeah, Elmer, don't let her buffalo yer!" hollered another man.

His words seemed to throw Elmer Keener into a rage. He growled, jerked the slack rein out of the woman's hand, started to back the buggy up. The buggy twisted and the woman swayed on the seat, trying hard not to fall from her perch.

"Miss Smarty Pants, how you like it now?" drawled one old boy.

Gunn dropped his gear, strode up to Elmer, jerked the reins from his hand. He grabbed the man by the collar, dragged him along as he carried the rein back to where the woman sat. He handed the leather strap to her, doffed his hat.

"Here you are, ma'am," he said pleasantly.

Elmer Keener took a swing at the tall man.

Gunn twisted him around, cocked a boot and planted it square on the man's rump. Elmer Keener reeled toward the gang on the boardwalk, crashed into them. They scattered.

One man stood up, evidently the leader.

"You done bought into trouble," he said.

Gunn's pale blue eyes turned slate grey as he fixed the man with a look.

The man carried two pistols on his belt, the butts turned face out. Army style. He was young, hard, clean-shaven, with dark nut-hard eyes, hair cut short under his battered hat. His clothes were not new, but they were tight on his muscled frame. He had a blunt nose like a hammer's ball, and his thin lips stretched across uneven teeth.

The woman held the reins, watching the unspoken challenge between the two men.

"Didn't catch your name," said Gunn.

"His name is Wayne Simons," said the woman. "Be careful."

Jed started to back away as Simons dropped his hand. They floated over the butts of his pistols like hovering kingfishers.

"I don't like to see a woman picked on," said Gunn. "Especially by a drunken out like that Elmer there."

Elmer blinked, scratched the knot on his head. The knot was new, developed when his head had struck the edge of the boardwalk. His eyes teetered in their sockets like loose beads in a bowl.

"I can handle my own troubles, Mister," said the woman.

Elmer Keener smirked, cocked his head and tried to focus on Gunn.

"All right," said Gunn, turning from the

boardwalk. "I'll leave you to it."

Elmer forced himself up by pushing with his hands. He stood there, swaying for a moment and then ran toward Gunn, rushing him with bowed neck, head down. He tackled Gunn from behind. Both men went down as the horse skittered backwards. A roar of laughter rose up from the bunch of men on the boardwalk.

"Look at old Elmer go!" said one.

"Sic him. Elmer. Bite his *cojones* off!"

Gun spit out a teaspoonful of dust and rolled away. Elmer staggered to his feet, tottered. He rushed Gunn, who was still sitting in the street, head lowered again like a ram in the rut. Gunn tried to rise, but the burly man bowled him over.

Air rushed from Gunn's lungs as Keener smashed into his midriff. His head rapped hard against the ground. Lights danced in his brain.

Stunned, Gunn opened his mouth, gasped for breath. He drew in dust, gagged, felt his stomach turn. Keener's weight was on his belly. Gunn brought up a knee. It caught Keener in the chest.

Elmer grunted, fell away.

Gunn struggled to his feet.

He was mad. His eyes seemed to be smoking. He clenched his fists, unclenched them. Jed was looking at him, an expression of curiosity on his face.

"Elmer," Gunn panted, "you sure do push a man hard."

"Mister Keener to you," said Elmer, bounding to his feet. The tussle had sobered him somewhat, apparently, because he waded into Gunn, both fists cocked.

Gunn waited for him.

There was no hurry.

Keener was showing off for the crowd. Others had

10

gathered to watch the fight as word had spread to the two saloons. The woman sat in her body, transfixed, her hand holding the reins lightly. The horse looked at the two men wall-eyed, ready to prance away if they came near.

Keener waddled closer, moving his fists in the air as if they were magic balls.

Gun's expression told him nothing. Hard slate eyes, lips curled in a half-smile. A vein in Gunn's neck pulsed like a blue snake.

Keener should have thought about that. About the way Gunn stood there, relaxed, waiting, his hands and arms perfectly relaxed. Instead, Keener toddled closer, bouncing those balled fists in the air.

He swung, missed.

Gunn's head was there one moment. The next it was gone.

Keener swung again, with the other fist.

Off-balance, he saw only a shadow. The shadow came at him from three feet away and got bigger and bigger until fireworks exploded in his head.

Gunn drew back all the way and plowed his fist into Keener's jaw with all the force of a piledriver. He felt his fist smack into bone. Saw Keener's head snap back as his nose exploded like a ripe tomato. Blood spewed. There was the sound of a sickening crunch, as knuckles crushed bone.

Keener dropped like a sack of spuds, blood spewing from his mangled nose.

Wayne Simons stepped off the boardwalk into the street.

The woman set the brake on the buggy, wrapped the reins around the wooden handle. She stood up to see over the horse's head.

Gunn caught the movement out of the corner of his eye, stepped away from the groveling drunk. Keener moaned, raised hands to his nose, trying to stem the bleeding. A pool of blood formed in the dust of the street.

"Mister, I'm calling you out," said Simons.

Gunn watched Simons take a stance, float his hands over the pistol butts. The man wasn't a crossdraw artist. He was going to drag those hoglegs out ass backwards and flip them. Both of them.

"Shit fire," muttered Gunn.

"What say? I'm calling your ass. Go for it."

Gunn sighed, crossed his arms.

"Look, feller," he said. "The man was drunker'n seventeen dollars. He'll heal likely. Buy you a drink in the hotel bar before we all cook in the sun."

Simon wasn't having any of it.

His lips, thin as dough crusts, curled in a snarl.

"No. You done took out one of my partners, Mister. You stuck your damned nose in, now you gotta get it out."

Gunn sighed again. The other men with Simon watched him with glittering eyes. There was a tension you could cut with a knife. The woman stood there in the buggy, like a statue.

It was worth one more try.

Death was just a fingersnap away. A man coud die on a San Antonio street in the middle of the afternoon and few would give a damn. The flies would come, soak up the blood, get sick on it, limber off with full bellies and let the undertaker come to cart him off. A swamper would throw some sawdust down or kick dirt on the dried blood and talk about it for twenty minutes over a beer. It was a hell of a way to cash in a good life. For no reason. For no good reason.

"Take your friend here and sober him up. He needs a doc, I'll pay the bill. He's hurtin' and I hate like hell to hit a drunk. I really do. But it's not worth dyin' over. If you take some time to think about it and still want to fight, come see me. The name's Gunn."

Gunn unfolded his arms.

"And," he continued, "if you want a drink, I'm buyin'."

The man who called himself Gunn let his arms hang down harmlessly at his side. He looked Simons square in the eye. Simons squinted. The men around him all looked up at him to see what he was going to do. There was a silence in the crowd of gapers. The silence was a claw-hammer hanging from a string. A silence of danger and promise as if a woman had walked among them carrying a Winchester. A silence like the lake ripples in a volcanic crater just before it erupts. A silence like the one a spider spins with its silken strands in cedar branches just before dusk.

And no one breathed.

For a long time.

Simon sucked in his breath. Broke the silence.

Gunn stood there, an odd light flickering in his pewter-grey eyes. A light that was shadow, mostly cloud. A light that was dense, startling, elusive, like the light a marsh flickers when the moon is high and the low fog moves in with a smothering cloak.

"You blab a lot, Mister," said Wayne Simons. "I ain't havin' no drink with you." He looked to his companions for support. They all nodded. Simons drew himself up proud, encouraged by the drinking men there on the boardwalk.

"What do you want, Simons?"

"Satisfaction, Mister."

Gunn's gaze did not waver.

Betsy, in the buggy, drew in a breath, held it.

Elmer Keener tried to sober up while his heart throbbed in his chest like a beheaded chicken.

The bunch up on the boardwalk tried to melt into

13

the wall of the falsefront saloon.

An onlooker coughed into his handkerchief, flushed with embarrassment.

A dog yapped down the street.

The horse hooked to the buggy nickered with a faint wavering ribbon of fear. Cocked its left hind hoof. Bobbed its head up and down.

One woman on the edge of the crowd sucked in a sob.

Insects buzzed, were heard suddenly, as if a thousand fiddlers had begun sawing away from afar. Even the buildings on the street seemed to crouch, bend forward.

Gunn saw it all. Heard it. Felt it.

"All right," said the man called Gunn. "Have it your way, feller. You call it."

Simons didn't even blink.

His hands flashed. He was fast. The fastest hands Gunn had ever seen.

A million moments went by in the wink of an eye.

Gunn's eye.

The moments were all bad. All eternal. Like drowning in a swamp, or drinking alkali water on the Mojave or looking straight down a mountain in winter when the snow was up to a man's armpits. A million quick moments. A hard knife in the groin. A bullet straight through the eyeball.

Simons was fast.

Very fast.

He drew the twin pistols out, brought them to bear even as he cocked them both with practiced thumbs.

Everyone saw it.

Gunn saw his life, his own life, ready to be blasted away.

He saw everything in a single moment.

Even those two barrels coming up and aiming at

14

him. Simons' thumbs cocking them on the rise, like an expert shooter.

Saw his death in those dark snouts.

Saw his death spouting from a gun barrel, as final as a rattlesnake's bite.

Saw his death like a blossoming orange flower.

Gunn was too slow.

He knew it. He fought against it.

But Simons was fast.

And the crowd stood up to see the stranger, Gunn, killed. They muttered words of hatred in their throats. They called, in Spanish and English, for the bull to be slain.

"Gunn, don't . . ." cried Jed Randall. "You can't make it. . . !"

Simons steadied his pistols, squeezed the triggers.

The smile on his lips was thin, raw as a slicing knife across a man's throat.

Gunn did not think.

He knew it would be close.

He knew, too, that he might die.

CHAPTER TWO

Betsy Masters had seen death up close. Lived with it. Thought about it day and night for years.

Death was sometimes sudden.

Sometimes, death carried a name with it. A soul.

Death was a horrible fact of life.

She looked at Gunn and saw it spread like a shadow all over him as he stood in the center of the street.

Clawing for his pistol.

She saw him dying there in the dirt, his skull stripped of flesh, his grey-blue eyes staring glassy at the sun. Saw his manly body shrivel like a stung plum, turn black as a shadowed berry.

His face, she knew, would frost over, turn rigid. His eyes would fix and gloss over like shiny marble buttons. Glass over like a frozen mountain stream. His muscles would stiffen and he'd be loaded in a wagon and carted away like buffalo calf carcass.

She swore. In her mind she swore.

A stranger, a man who did not know her, had defended her. Had taken up her cause.

And now, he was about to die.

Gunn. This hawkfaced man who had come to her rescue, fought for her with a passion that thrilled her.

It was almost too much for her to bear.

Betsy lifted her hands to her face. She shuddered, buried her face in her palms, unable to watch Wayne Simons shoot down the stranger.

Simons brought out steel guns. Leather creaked and whispered and groaned. Like a door opening. Sun flashed on pistol barrels.

Gunn cleared leather before Simons could turn his wrists.

His thumb cocked the hammer on the Colt. Smooth, effortless. The hammer slid back as the barrel rose.

Gunn focused his attention on one wrist. He pictured the angle, saw the ball of lead streak to its target. He saw the shot clearly before he shot.

His finger squeezed the trigger with a gentle tug as the barrel leveled.

Perfect motion. Perfect control.

The Colt bucked in Gunn's hand.

Simons and his pistols angled symmetrically, V-shaped a half foot from his belt.

Orange flame and grey smoke belched from the barrel of the Colt.

The .44 ball slammed into Simons' wrist. The right wrist. Bone snapped, blood vessels burst and spewed twin spouts from their smashed tubes.

Simons screamed.

The fingers of his right hand spasmed, contracted as if he'd touched a hot stove lid. The pistol dropped from his grasp, thudded to the dirt. His left hand, stalled from the symmetry of his draw, from a lack of coordination, turned rigid as stone.

A man can think of only one thing at a time.

Simons felt a shoot of pain course up his right arm. The pain scrambled his brain, numbed his senses. Pure pain, like a clean splinter driven up under the fingernail. Pain like a knife pressing into the heart or slicing across the throat. Pain like a maul smashing into a sore finger. That kind of hard clean pain. Straight to the brain. Stopping everything else.

Simons screamed. Involuntarily. And the scream was clean and raw, too, like a scalping knife parting the hair from a skull.

Lights danced just behind Simons' eyes.

The man who shot him dulled to a blur, shimmered there in the street, out of focus.

The pain streaked up and down his arm, dazzled his brain, razored his groin, twisted his intestines into hard throbbing knots.

A man next to Simons thought about going for it. His hand moved six inches toward the pistol on his hip.

But the man looked at Gunn, at the smoking Colt steady in the man's hand. He thought of centuries in a single instant. He thought of blood and pain and the dark lonely if he went down with a bullet in his heart. He thought of everything he liked about life in that

17

one instant and of how close and deep the ground was at that moment.

The man froze his hand, dipped his head. Defeated.

The crowd froze, too, like a clutch of sculptures, all bone white and scared, struck with awe at the quickness of Gunn's shot, its terrible accuracy. Squeaks and squeals and whines issued from their throats.

Gunn looked at the dead pistol on the ground. The useless, wasted pistol that had not been fired, could not fire without a hand to hold it. His own pistol dipped and he hammered back, squeezed. The pistol on the ground clanged with a leaden spang, spun through the dust.

Gunn thumbed the hammer back, made the twirling pistol dance and skitter for several inches.

Then Gunn leveled his pistol at Simons again. He eased the hammer back slow. The sound of cocking was loud. Clean and loud, as the gear engaged. It was the sound of a prison cell slamming shut. The sound of a trapdoor banging as the lever was pulled. The sound of sudden death . . . waiting.

"The next one goes into your mouth, Simons," said Gunn quietly.

Simons dropped to one side. Blood blew out of his arm like a crimson fountain.

"Jeeee-*sus!*" he exclaimed, his face paling.

His left hand opened. The second pistol plummeted from his hand. The weapon thumped on the ground, lay still as a dead snake.

Gunn eased the hammer back down on the Colt.

He shoved the pistol back in its holster.

"Ma'am," he said, tipping his hat, and strolled back to his gear, picked it up. "Come on, Jed. Let's get us a bunk."

"You like the forty-four better?"

"Yeah," said Gunn. "It is some kind of pistol."

"Too much gun, though. Could break a wrist." Randall built a smoke, waited while Gunn rubbed his neck after the shave.

"You have to put wrist in it. Push it when you squeeze."

"I never saw anything like that in my life. The people just backed on out of there. And Simons, he was white as a bleached sheet."

"Simons is one of those."

"Huh?"

Gunn squinted in the mirror, smoothed back his hair on the sides. His hair was too long, but it kept the sun from baking his pate and stayed in place when it was gritty with sand and dust and woodsmoke. He had washed it out and now loose strands strayed all over his head. His face looked different. Like a peeled onion. He stuck out his tongue, turned to Randall, who was sitting bassackwards on a chair.

"Simons. Gets two guns. Two cavalry holsters. Cuts off the flaps. Puts some fancy handles on the pistols. Hangs 'em low. Look deadly as hell. He figures to scare shit out of everyone comes up against him. But it takes time to turn those wrists the wrong way, pull the iron out of the holsters, then flip the hoglegs into position. Cock, fire. Hell, you could have taken him, Jed."

Jed pushed the chair away, stood up.

"He was fast, Gunn. Damned fast."

"Yeah, he was. He just had too many things to do. Simple is better."

Jed laughed, but he didn't know what he was laughing at. They were all slicked up and going down to the hotel bar.

Simons had friends.

Some of them might be drunked up, waiting for Gunn to show up.

"We could send out for some grub," said Randall. "Pay a *mozo* to fetch some tortillas, frijoles, beef."

"We could hide out like kangaroo rats and steal at night, too."

"Shit fire, Gunn, you rubbed some people plumb raw."

Gunn said nothing. His pale blue eyes faded to a smoke grey as he trimmed the wick in the lamp, blew it out.

Jed stumbled through the dark to the door, but Gunn was already in the hall, heading for the stairs.

Jed closed the door, locked it. He cursed as he discovered that his hands were shaking.

"Hey, wait for me," he said, hurrying away from the door as if afraid to be left alone. Gunn gave a man that feeling, though. He walked a straight line sometimes and kept his big thoughts to himself. It was damned aggravating.

Going down the stairs, Jed kept staring at the new .44 Colt on Gunn's hip.

It looked big. Almost like an advertisement painted on a barn.

CHEW CLIMAX TOBACCO.

"What was that you said?" Jed asked, as he caught up to Gunn. "About pushing it when you squeeze. The forty-four."

Gunn kept going, talking over his shoulder.

"A plow handle in your hands, Jed. You just shove it hard. If you hit a stump or a clump or a rock, you keep pushing. Same as the forty-four. It bucks in your hand, you keep your aim steady if you push."

"You make it sound so damned simple."

Gunn laughed. Then, he stopped abruptly, turned

to look up at Randall.

"You stay on top of your gun," he said, "or it'll turn against you everytime. It'll back you into a corner if you let it. It'll turn on you if you let it. Savvy? You push it and hold it down lest it rise up and smite you."

"You talk Bible stuff?"

"I talk a straight brand. Now quit talking about the things that scare you white and let the kink out of your rope. There are tools and tools. A big bore pistol is just another tool, only bigger."

"Yeah?"

"Yeah," Gunn smirked, "and bigger is sometimes better."

He laughed, lunged at Jed. Jed fell back on the stairs, startled.

"See them big hands?" Gunn teased, moving his fingers like children do when trying to frighten one another.

Then he dropped the next few steps to the lobby, walking tall past the gaping people sitting in wood chairs.

The hotel bar was busy at that hour of the evening. Lamps glowed with flickering orange flames. The windows were a cool blue-black as dusk enveloped the sky, the earth. Voices chattered in crepuscular murmurings, glasses tinked with mellow bell sounds. Blue streamers of smoke hung in the air, like thin wisps of clouds. The smells of tobacco, from cigars, spittoon and cigarettes assaulted Gunn's nostrils with a tangy musty clutch on his senses. Civilization. Men and women talking, laughing, trying to pack a lifetime into a few moments. The scent of whiskey and beer, *mezcal, tequila* and bad breath permeated the close air inside the bustling bar.

Gunn ordered whiskies, stood with his foot on the rail.

He and Jed eyed the men drinking at the bar sitting at tables scattered about the large room.

They listened to the conversations, trying to make sense out of them as they sipped their drinks. The whiskey burned raw down Gunn's throat, warmed his belly.

" 'Member old Sykes," said one man, "when we runnin' on the Cimmaron last fall?"

"Yep. Sure do."

"Broke his leg durin' a stampede got tromped into the prairie."

They head talk of "buff" and "buff'ler."

"You got it figgered out, Gunn?" asked Jed.

"Somewhat. Hide hunters, I reckon."

A man turned to Gunn, his wall-eyes glaring.

"Hide hunters? Mister, we're buff runners."

"Yeah," said Jed drily. "Buffalo hunters."

The grizzled man in the buckskins gave a snort, squinted one eye almost shut and seemed to be able to puff out the other eye until it was enormous.

"Buffalo hunters my ass," he bellowed. "Only a rank greenhorn ever calls hisself a buffalo hunter. We run 'em, pilgrim, and we're the best they is!"

Gunn looked at the man. He was thick in the shoulders, top-heavy, but his legs were sturdy, bowed so much if he'd stood straight he'd be four inches taller. He wore a thick curly beard, streaked with grey, a leather hat, carried a big skinning knife next to his enormous pistol.

"Saw you out there earlier, defendin' the lady," he added. "The name's Charlie Danvers, but they call me 'Curly Cow' Danvers. Curly cow, now that's another name fer buff."

"What are you all doin' here?" asked Gunn.

"Waitin' fer word. Expeditions goin' out any day now. They's money to be made and spent. They's hides to skin, buff to shoot."

"Lot of people in town," observed Jed. "What outfit you going with?"

"Might hire on with Masters. He's the best. Thet gal out there you stood up for was one of John Masters' daughters. He's got two of 'em. Laura and Betsy. Purtiest gals around. Both go on the expeditions, too, 'long with their ma. Cook up a mighty fine stew. Masters' bunch is the only buff runners I know of what has women folk along. John's wife, Evie, rides right out there with him. Hard place for a woman, though."

Gunn looked closely at Curly Cow Danvers. The man's eyes were blue, steaked with red. His nose was bulbous, pocked. Underneath the beard, he could make out a scar or two.

"Any reason why that Elmer Keener was pickin' on Betsy?" asked Gunn.

"Competition. Keener works for the Simons brothers. They run an outfit outta here. Keener's a good skinner. They don't like Masters much. He generally beats 'em to ever' herd out there. And thet Betsy, why she shot five bulls in the last big herd while Keener missed two cows that run from the same pack."

"Thought you said he was a skinner," said Jed.

"When you're suckin' hind tit, you shoot too, 'till the skinnin' starts."

Gunn laughed.

"I'll buy you a drink old-timer. What's your preference?"

"Why thet good whiskey you boys are swallerin' would do just fine. Better whiskey here than most places."

"So Keener was mad that the gal bested him," said Gunn.

23

"More than that. The Simons boys lost their asses and a good part of their shirt on the last run."

"These buffalo runners must take their business right seriously," said Gunn.

"Dead seriously," said Danvers.

Gunn finished his whiskey, ordered another round. Danvers was a talkative man, said he used to hunt with Frank Mayer, a legendary hunter.

"John Masters is a lot like Frank—John's a mite older. Frank's about your age. What'd you say your name was?"

"Gunn."

"Just Gunn?" The old man tugged at his beard as if trying to remember something. "I heard of a Gunnison up in Coloraddy. Changed his name to Gunn. 'Course this was Bill Gunnison, fought with the 24th Wisconsin at Missionary Ridge. That was a fight."

Gunn swallowed some of his drink. The old days were not always best.

Jed cleared his throat, said nothing. He knew how Gunn had lost his wife. Laurie, gone after the men involved in her rape. Killed them or sent them to prison. And lately one of the men had surfaced again, broken out of prison. Gunn had killed him. So the past was buried. Or was it? Gunn had never remarried, had stayed to the long trails, unwilling to settle down. He could see that Gunn was interested in Danvers' accounts of buff running. Something like that might appeal to Gunn. There were few things he hadn't done, but hunting buffalo was one of them.

"Well, Gunn's name enough. And you, young feller?"

"Jed Randall. We just delivered some beeves to the post."

"Dull work. Runnin' buff's the thing. Dangerous as

24

hell. You got Injuns to contend with and plenty of competition. Feller shoots as good as you do, ought to do well. Masters pays better'n most. Better'n Simons, at least."

Gunn started to say something when a buckskin-clad young man came up to him.

"You Gunn?"

Gunn nodded.

"Just wanted to give a word to the wise, seein' you're a friend of Curly Cow Charlie's."

"This here's Nat Wales," said Danvers. "He's a friend. What you got in yore poke, Nat?"

"Wayne Simons is plenty mad. He's makin' smoke across the street about how he's going to stretch out your hide."

"He had his chance," said Gunn.

Danvers squinted both eyes.

"It ain't Wayne you got to worry about," he said softly.

"No," agreed Wales. "His brothers are plumb mad their little brother got ridiculed in public like that."

"Brothers?" gulped Jed Randall.

"Yair," said Danvers. "Forgot to tell you about thet. Wayne's plenty mean, but he's tame compared to Kurt and Lefty. Them's his brothers. They're the worst to come down the pike. You stay clear. They don't know any way but dirty in a fight."

Gunn smiled.

"Think I'll turn in early," he said. "Jed?"

"I'll stay a while. The talk's gettin' interestin'."

Gunn walked through the saloon. Eyees followed him. After he left, a man near the door, rose from his chair, went outside. He crossed the street in a hurry.

His name was Wally Burns and he worked for Claude Simons, the father of Wayne, Lefty and Kurt. He went inside the Red Dog, a few doors down, where he knew the Simons boys would buy him a drink, listen to what he had to say.

CHAPTER THREE

Gunn hung up his gunbelt, lay on the bed. He'd put away a steak, beans, a half dozen biscuits, a quarter pot of coffee. Through the open window he could hear the sounds drifting up the street from the saloons. Juniper Street never seemed to slow down. There were at least five bars, including the hotel's, a cantina wedged in between a tack store and a gun dealer. He was weary, but not sleepy. It might be best to stay inside, let some tempers cool. He had no wish to tangle with the Simons brothers. They'd get it all talked out, forget about it by morning when they had their hangovers to keep them distracted.

He sat up, built a smoke, tossed the makings on the table next to the ashtray. The lamp threw an orange glow on the table, kept the shadows at bay.

Shadows. they were still there. After all these years. Since Laurie's death. Since Coker and his bunch raped her, left her to die. Now, it had come up again. With Danvers.

Yes, he had used to be William Gunnison. He had fought in the War Between the States. At Missionary Ridge. But that was another man. And the man who had met and married Laurie was still another man. He had tried to erase the past. Changed his name. As if shedding skin. Gunnison to Gunn. She had called him Billy, but he didn't want anyone to call him that anymore. So, just Gunn. It was a neutral name. A new name to let people know he had dropped a lot of baggage back there in Colorado. Simplified his life. No roots. No past. Just the present. That was enough. That was the only time a man could live anyway. He couldn't live in the past. It was already gone. He couldn't live in the future. It hadn't arrived yet. He could only live in the Now. The present. A single moment at a time.

But Laurie was still there in the shadows. Now. Even though she had gone. Was dead. He felt her presence at times like these. In empty hotel rooms with the oil lamp flickering, noises from the street. People talking, drinking, laughing. The towns were all strange to him now. Faceless, like the men he had killed. The old trails gone dim, fading from memory. The next trail uncertain. So many places to go, so many things yet to do that he hadn't done before. But always riding away from the past, from that burned down ranch up on the Poudre, from that lonely grave where Laurie lay in peaceful repose.

He got up, punched out the cigarette in the ashtray. Ground it down to shreds, the tobacco still smouldering.

The knock on the door startled him.

He strode to the nail where his pistol hung, grabbed the butt of the Colt.

"Who's there?"

"Betsy Masters."

Gunn relaxed his grip on the pistol, let his hand fall away.

"Be right with you."

He opened the door. She looked smaller than she had earlier that day. About five and a half feet. Her hair was down over her shoulders. She wore a fresh dress, a pale purple. A matching ribbon in her hair.

"May I come in?" she asked, as if she needed his

permission. She went right by him before he could answer. He closed the door, locked it, out of habit. She surveyed the room, turned, took off her bonnet. She carried a small handbag, which she deposited, along with her bonnet, on the dresser.

"Yeah. Come on in," Gunn said drily.

She laughed and dimples appeared on her cheeks like the holes doodlebugs burrow in soft sand. She had even white teeth. Her eyes sparkled. Her laugh was low, throaty.

"I wanted to thank you for standing up for me today."

"It wasn't anything." Gunn stood there.

"Aren't you going to offer me a chair?"

"I'm sorry. Sit down anywhere."

"What about you?"

There were two chairs. They were both by the table. Close together. She made him very nervous. She was a young woman and had come to his hotel room late at night. In some places, that would not be exactly proper.

She laughed again, sat in a chair. Gunn hesitated, then crossed the room. He pulled the empty chair away from the table. She sat primly, regarding him.

"You have grey eyes."

"Well, blue. Sort of."

"No, they're grey. I had a cat once with grey eyes."

He stopped looking at her eyes. He moved his chair farther away from her.

"Do you know where the Masters place is?"

"No," he admitted.

"I told my father about you. He was in town earlier, talked to some men. He said he'd like to see you. Tomorrow."

"What are you doing walking around a town like this, a street like this, late at night?"

She laughed again, crossed her legs. He saw a flash of ankle. Very trim.

"I'm staying here at the hotel, silly. I had business until late, didn't feel like riding back with my pa. All I had to do was walk down one door."

"You're staying here?"

"Right next door. I stay here all the time."

"How old are you?"

"Twenty. Why?"

"Ma'am, this is one of the roughest streets I've ever been on. You almost got a man killed today. And you're staying in one of the worst hotels I've ever been in. It doesn't make sense."

"Oh, you're very wrong, Gunn. Is that your whole name? Yes, I guess it is. I stay here because this is where we outfit the expeditions. I know you talked to Curly Cow Charlie tonight because he told me so. And he's coming out tomorrow. You and your friend can ride out with him. He knows the way. We're outfitting for the next buffalo hunt. If you're not a coward, and I don't think you are, my father might make you an offer."

"I don't know anything about shooting buffalo."

"What do you hunt, Gunn? Men? Women?"

She leaned forward, a serious expression on her face. Her voice was husky in her throat.

"I hunt meat when I have to."

"You backed Wayne Simons down. That's something. His whole bunch is a little bit afraid of you if you want the truth."

"I wouldn't know. I just tried to keep from killing the man, that's all."

"Man? Compared to you, he's just a boy."

"All right."

He didn't want to argue with her. She was after something. He just couldn't figure it out. But she made him very uncomfortable.

"All right, what?"

"All right, he's just a boy. And you're just a girl. And it's late, Miss Masters."

"What about tomorrow? Will you come out? Mister Randall has already agreed."

"Jed? You talked to him?"

"Of course. He's the one who gave me your room number."

"Jed's a cattleman. He doesn't know anything about buffalo."

"He can shoot, use a knife. He's young, tough."

Gunn knew the only way he was going to get rid of her was to agree to come out and talk to her father. Buffalo was Indian meat. Big, lumbering beasts, he could not imagine going out shooting them. Running them. It would be like shooting cattle. Or trees.

"I'll go out there with Jed and Danvers. But I'm not very interested."

"What would make you interested?"

She got up, came close to him. Her breasts were at eye level. He looked up, into her eyes. Her brown eyes flickered with promise, desire.

"I thought you were going to be killed today. Simons would have killed you. I felt badly because you stood up for me. When you backed him down, I felt something else. You didn't stay around long enough for me to thank you. But I haven't been able to get you out of my mind."

"Ma'am . . . I . . ."

"I saw Wayne pushing you. Now I'm pushing you. You're stubborn as an old mule."

Gunn felt trapped. She moved still closer. He squirmed. Her hands shot out, grabbed his face. Impulsively, she leaned down, kissed him. Her mouth locked on his. Her lips crushed his own.

And then her tongue flicked inside his mouth.

He felt a spear of pleasure stab through his loins.

He grabbed her then, slammed her down in his lap. He wrapped his arms around her, threw her head back and kissed her hard. He rammed his tongue inside her mouth, probed her lips, her tongue, the roof of her mouth. She squirmed in his arms, but returned his tongue-probe with one of her own. She opened her mouth and he could feel the heat. Her lips were wet, slippery, yielding. And a fire raged in him.

"Hold me, hold me tight," she moaned. Her mouth opened to take his tongue again.

Gunn stared at her, his eyes narrowing.

Felt her flesh in his arms, her weight on his lap. The tugging strain at his trousers as his manhood grew, flushed stiff with blood.

"You are a woman," he husked. "A wildcat."

She strained, pushing her lips toward his. Wet lips, glistening in the lamp glow. Mouth open, tongue bobbing between them like a cobra. Hypnotic as sin. Gunn met her halfway, tasted her again. Tasted the fire, felt it stream down to his groin. She squirmed in his arms, pressed her buttocks against he swollen stalk rising out of his lap, stretching his trousers into a tent.

The kiss between them was savage, an exchange of heat and steam, stabbing tongues, torrid breaths. When they broke, she panted, gazed up into his pale pewter eyes.

"Blue," she said, "blue as dawn."

"Betsy, you asked for it and now it's too late for me to back down. Twenty, you say? Not a virgin I hope."

"No. Does it make any difference?"

"Not a bit."

"I want you inside me. I'm all wet. My panties are soaked."

"Don't talk like that, child."

"I'm not a child! I'm a woman. Full growed."

"Umm. I don't know. Not yet."

"I can feel you underneath me. You're hard. Hard as a rock." She moved her buttocks, teased the swollen tip of his cock. He felt the crease, the gap between the twin hemispheres. His cock hardened even more.

"Betsy, you don't tease a man."

"I'm not teasing. Take me. See."

He hefted her in his arms, stood up. Walked to the bed, threw her down. The bed bounced. Wooden slats creaked with the strain.

"Take off your clothes," he gruffed. "Don't linger none."

"No," she rasped, her voice a low purr in her throat. Her eyes watched him as he stripped out of his shirt, unbuckled his belt, slid trousers down lean hard legs. His stalk sprang into view as she slid her damp panties down sleek legs glowing bronze in the light.

"My, my. Big. You felt big."

He looked at her legs drawn together chastely, cramping her nest.

"Don't ever tease a man, Betsy. And when you spark a fire, don't shovel any sand on it." He paused. "Spread your legs."

A shocked look hardened her face. He smiled at her, started toward her, his bowed cock bouncing with every step. The head glistened with seeping oils, swayed, dipped, rose in the air. She softened then, her eyes fixed on the flared head of the cobra, the mushroomed crown slick with the fluid of desire.

"Gunn, oh, Gunn," she breathed. "I want it, want it so much . . . I won't tease you . . . just let me have it . . ."

Her legs widened into a vee, exposing the triangular vee, the thatch and its swollen slit, puffy with yearning.

Gunn slid onto the bed, onto her body, pressing her down with his weight. He kissed her again. A hand squeezed her breast. A finger teased her nipple. She began undulating, seeking his throbbing cock, but he kept the tip poised against the lips of her cleft.

"You're teasing me," she sighed.

"Only enough, and for good reason."

"I want you . . . want you inside me."

"You'll want me more in a few minutes. Patience, Betsy. A man goes quick. A woman goes often and long."

"How do you know so much?"

He eased down, took a nipple in his mouth, worried it with his tongue. She arched her back, oozed dampness between her legs. She pounded fists on his back. He teased the nipple until it stood up hard as a thumb. Her thighs began to buck, slamming up against him.

"Gunn you—you've got me so hot," she breathed.

He pulled himself atop her, looked down into dark eyes. Eyes that swam with moisture, wanting. Eyes that tugged at him with their wanton light.

She reached out, impulsively, grasped his stalk with her hand. Tightened around it. Felt its pulse. Its blood-throb in her palm. He kissed her forehead, dipped his loins.

She released him, felt the first push of his cock.

"Relax," he said. "Let it slide in."

"Ooooh, you know what to say; what to do."

He slid inside.

She writhed with pleasure. The folds of her sex parted like some evening flower, dewy with rivermist. He slid through the pulsating folds of bubbling flesh, the sensitive tip of his organ probing the core of her.

Betsy touched his sinewy arms, ran her hands up and down them.

Before he reached his depth, she buckled with pleasure. Her body spasmed. Waves of electric sensation coursed through her. Her mouth opened. She screamed softly. Screamed again as an orgasm shot a tingling bullet through her thighs. Her hands jerked on his arms, found his back. Fingernails scraped his flesh like cat's claws, not digging deep, but scratching, just the edges touching. Her legs rose up in the air, knees contracted, and she rocked with him as he plumbed her loins, stroking in and out of her scalding tunnel with slow, sure strokings.

Each stroke furrowing brought the fire to life. Each stroke furrowing made her buck until she danced on the bed with a mindless thrashing rhythm. The climaxes concatenated, furrowed into one another until all of her nerve ends were like a map of rivers and streams, all screaming at once, jangling like electrified keys at the end of a kite string during a thunderstorm.

Gunn waited until she was writhing so hard on the bed he had to pin her down by the hips with his hands. He cupped her buttocks, brought her up to him as he undulated his hips slowy, then fast. Timing her climaxes, timing his own thrusts.

"Come, come," she moaned. "I want you to come. Now . . ."

And that was the moment.

The right moment.

He played her slow, like a trout dance-flipping on the end of a line. Like a thrashing bass trying to shake the hook. He drove into her with hard thrusts and slid slow on the back-thrust.

And when she rose with him, he rose with her. Clear to the top, the pinnacle. Past the high peaks, over the summit until she exploded into a frenzied thrashing and his seed burst with a milky spewing splatter. And he held himself deep as her body quickened its rhythms, clutched him at the thighs, until he was drained and she was full of his seed.

"It was a godly thing," she panted, her body sleek with their mingled sweats. "A truly godly thing."

Gunn was silent, catching his breath.

He had beaten off the shadows. He looked down at her glowing body, felt himself spewing out, limp, stated, spent. She was golden, brown-eyed, purring.

They lay there, basking in the lampglow, catching their breaths, snaring back their flown senses.

She got up, later, surprising him. He reached for the makings, sat up, his sweat dried on his skin.

"You're leaving?"

"I must. Pa always sends someone to ckeck on me at midnight."

"Cinderella."

"I'm sorry. You made me very happy, Gunn. I love your name. I love your—every thing about you."

"I'll come out tomorrow," he said, sad that she was leaving.

"Come early. Claude Simons has already spread the word he's looking for you."

"Wayne Simons' father?"

"Yes. And his sons, Lefty and Kurt. When they sober up, they'll come gunning for you."

"I won't run from them."

"No, I know you won't. But they'll shoot you in the back anyway. Even if you're looking them straight in the eye."

Gunn looked at her soberly. A cold chill crawled up his back.

She dressed quickly, kissed him before she left. He watched her hurry down the hall to the next room. Heard her door close. He closed his own. The makings were still in his hand. He didn't want a smoke now.

He wanted Betsy.

And he wished he'd never come to San Antonio.

CHAPTER FOUR

John Masters stood on the porch of his log cabin home watching the mist hold on the land. It had been dry, then wet. Hot, then cool. Now it was sultry, even at that hour of the morning and there was a haze over the pasture that lingered like campfire smoke.

He was a big, rawboned hunk of a man, whose face was florid, lined with tiny red rivers from taking too much drink. His shoulders were broad, his torso lean and tapered. He sported a hairy chest, brushy moustache, thick hair with only a centered bald spot to indicate his true age.

He held a steaming mug of coffee in his hand, took in deep breaths. He did not smoke, but took tobacco at times, especially during the hunt. That kept his thirst down, his nerves up, keen. Now, he slaked his thirst on the steaming coffee, blew on the liquid to keep from scalding his lips. His nose was straight, his eyes set far apart, brown as coffee. He wore mocassined boots, tight buckskin trousers that could barely contain his thighs, an open muslin shirt with bulky sleeves that did not hinder his muscular arms.

"Mighty fine morning," he said, as a meadowlark trilled in the field.

His wife Evie came through the door, stood beside him, as if she had been waiting for him to speak. She was a tall, stately woman, younger than he, younger looking than she was, with fine light hair, deep brown eyes, squared-off cheek bones and chin. She carried a bottle of *mezcal* in her hand.

"Did you want to sweeten your coffee, John?"

"Yes. I'll have a touch."

He drank a tot of *mezcal* in his coffee every morning. He said it was good for the blood. He ate no breakfast, usually. He always said a man on an empty stomach was a better hunter. The alcohol, he thought, gave his senses an even keener edge. John Masters lived for hunting and even when he was home, he hunted in his mind.

John was born in 1838 in Ohio. He left home at an early age, worked his way west, dipped down into Mexico for a time before arriving in Texas. He went even farther west and north, but Texas drew him back. In San Antonio, he first heard about "buffalo running." Some men hunted from horseback, but the man he hooked up with shot from a stand and there was no running involved at all. After two seasons, he borrowed enough money to match his savings and bought a wagon. He hired a guide who loaned him a .50-.70 Army issue Sharps rifle. He began hunting buffalo in the spring of 1871 when he was thirty-three years old. He had Evie with him, and his two daughters. Evie did not mind travel, had given birth to Laura up in Wyoming when she was sixteen years old. That was in 1856. Laura was now 22, Betsy, born in Kansas, 20. The girls had learned to love buffalo meat, could help with the light butchering, the cooking. John was proud of his family, but he wondered how long he could keep hunting buffalo. Expenses were mounting and the herds were thinner, harder to find.

"Someone's coming," said Evie, pouring an ounce of *mezcal* into his cup.

"Betsy get in all right?"

"She and Laura are bathing down to the crick."

John saw the dust, squinted his eyes. Three riders.

"She say who was coming?'

"Curly Cow Charlie, those two strangers."

"Gunn. Randall. I hope Betsy's right about 'em."

"I wish we still had Jesse and Slim. They was good boys, John."

"The best."

Jesse had gotten bit by a rattlesnake the previous summer. Slim went blind in a fight that winter—his antagonist had thrown lye powder in his face. Buffalo runners were a hard lot. They lived hard, died hard. She had seen many of them come and go, thought of them as sons, almost. Daughters were fine, but she longed for a son. It was probably too late now for them. John, too, she knew, would have liked to have had a son. He was always spoiling his men, especially the younger ones.

The *mezcal* bit into John's stomach, burned like a hot branding iron. The aroma of the coffee and liquor drifted to his nostrils. It was a sweet morning. Men were coming who might ride up to Oklahoma territory with him. Curly Cow Charlie was all right, despite his age. He could still scamper. Danvers had once been a mountian man until the beaver had petered out. He had lived on buffalo more than any white man John knew.

"I'll see to the girls," said his wife. "They probably forgot to take robes with them."

John laughed.

They were not as modest as the girls had been in his day. Living the rough life, most of it in the outdoors, made them less self-conscious about their bodies. That was good and it was bad. On the trail, he'd had to give them stern warnings about what they showed around the men. "Too much leg or ankle after thirty days running buffalo," he said, "can drive a man plumb *loco.*" It was true. To the men he gave only one warning. "If I catch you in either of my daughters' blankets, you get hitched first town we hit." He suspected that Laura and Betsy had found ways around his rules, but he didn't know for sure. It was Evie he worried about anyway. He had not been able to do his husbandly duty for two winters now and, even though they slept together, he often heard her weeping at night because he could not quench the fires he knew burned in her loins. He had sewed too many wild oats as a young man, sleeping with squaws and Mexicans and had gotten the dripping sickness. Now, the doc had told him he was burned out.

He finished his coffee, the aftertaste of *mezcal* lingering in his mouth. He set the cup down, leaned against the post, watching the three dots loom larger as the horsemen approached. Behind him, leaning against the wall, was a big rifle, the one he had first borrowed, later bought from his old guide, a half-Cherokee named Jack Blood.

Gunn saw the man on the porch.

"That Masters?" he asked Danvers.

"That be he. Big feller, ain't he?"

"Big enough." He wondered what Masters would say if he knew Betsy had been in his room last night. He had awakened before dawn, knocked on her door, but she had already gone. He had rousted out Randall, who had a hangover as big as mountain. They had met Danvers in the lobby, had coffee at a café after saddling up.

Danvers reined up. Gunn and Randall followed suit. Gunn felt Masters sizing him up with eagle eyes.

"You Gunn?" he asked.

Gunn nodded.

"Hear you did some fancy shooting in town

39

yesterday."

"Not fancy. Just practical."

Masters laughed, a booming laugh that rolled out of his chest like thunder.

"Think you can handle a buffalo gun? I need some shooters."

Gunn suppressed a smile.

"I have shot rifles."

"Haw! Rifles!" Masters walked to the wall, snatched up the Sharps. "Climb down, boys, hitch your horses. Rifles! Haw!"

Danvers gave Gunn a sheepish look as the men wrapped reins around the hitch rail.

When Gunn stepped out, Masters threw him the Sharps.

Gunn looked at it, tried to read the caliber stamped into the barrel. It was almost smoothed out.

"It's a .50-.70 Sharps," said Masters. "See that *olla* on that stump? I set it out there this morning. It's exactly four hundred yards from where you're standing."

Masters pointed to a large earthen jug. He stepped down from the porch, stood towering over Gunn, who was a shade over six feet himself.

Gunn looked at the jug.

"Hell, I can't even see it at this distance," he said.

Some men drifted out from behind the house, drawn by Masters' booming laugh. They wore buckskins, looked rough-hewn.

"Uh oh," said one, a skinner named Bucky Meeks, "old John's brought out the Sharps. We got us a greenhorn."

The buckskinners lounged on the porch as Gunn hefted the rifle.

He held it to his shoulder, sighted down the barrel.

"How do you set these sights?"

40

"They're set. You just line it up the best way you know how, pilgrim, and squeeze the trigger. Curly Cow will watch you if you fall down."

The men on the porch guffawed. Randall looked around at them sheepishly.

"That bad, huh?" asked Gunn.

Gunn scowled, held the rifle up to his shoulder again. Cocked the big hammer. The rifle had a fifty caliber bore. The ball was shoved by 70 grains of black powder in a cartridge. He had shot more powder before in a fifty caliber. A hundred and ten grains once. The Sharps couldn't be worse.

He lined up the sights, dead center on the *olla*.

Squeezed the trigger while holding his breath.

The rifle boomed. A cloud of white smoke blasted out the barrel. The *olla* exploded, sending shards of pottery flying in all directions. The stock slammed into Gunn's shoulder. The cheek piece cracked against his face.

The men on the porch cheered.

"You'll do," said Masters, taking the rifle from Gunn. "Want to join my party? I pay good. Most outfits divide their profits, half to the hunter, half to the skinners, cooks, drivers and roustabouts. Me, I keep a quarter of the profits, turn the rest over to my men to split up equally. It works out a little sweeter."

"Sounds fine to me."

Masters slapped Gunn on the back, almost staggering him.

"You're on. Curly Cow?"

"I come to hunt with you, John."

"Fine, now what about this other feller. Randall? Can you shoot as good as your pardner?"

Randall grinned. The grin hurt. Everything hurt.

"Better," he said wryly. "I taught him."

"You look more like a skinner to me," said Masters,

41

looking Randall over. "Can you handle a knife without cutting off your own nuts?"

The men on the porch laughed again.

Randall blushed.

"I reckon."

"Fine. The expedition leaves day after tomorrow. I'm not a hard man to work for. I expect you to follow orders, take your places when we set up on a stand. I go along with Ben Franklin's words: 'If you ride a horse, sit close and tight. If you ride a man, sit easy and light.' "

Masters extended his big hand to Randall, then to Gunn. He shook each one's hand warmly.

"Bunkhouse is out back. The boys will find room for you. Bucky, you show these boys to the stables. Curly Cow, you know where everything is."

"John, you know I always sleep out."

"Just don't get stepped on. We got a lotta stock wanderin' around."

Gunn started to go for his horse, but Masters held him back with a hand on his shoulder.

"Want you to take supper with us this evenin', Gunn. I got some thankin' to do."

"It isn't necessary, Mister Masters."

"Call me John. No, the missus wants to meet you. And I expect my daughter Laura is some curious about you."

"I'm much obliged."

"See you at supper. I got a heap to do."

Masters walked to the house. Gunn watched him climb the steps. He liked the man. There was something open and honest about him. He wondered, though, if Betsy was good at keeping secrets. Even from her sister, Laura.

"Was he nice?"

"Laura, he was perfect." Betsy bobbed her torso into the stream like a duck. The water dribbled off her sleek skin. Her light brown hair darkened with the wetness, like a seal's hide. Her breasts floated on the water like melons.

"Nobody's perfect," pouted Laura. She was dark-haired, tall like her mother and father, with nut-brown eyes, an upturned nose, broad shoulders. She splashed water on her breasts, shivered in the cool drench of water. She stood slightly taller than her sister. Her dark thatch dripped as she climbed to the shore.

They heard the sound of laughter.

"Ooooh, they're here!" giggled Betsy.

Laura's eyes widened. Her eyebrows arched.

"Did you bring towels? Our robes?"

"Silly! Let the men see us. It won't hurt."

"Betsy, you are a caution! Mamma finds out what a tease you are, she'll pull your hair out by the roots."

Betsy stuck her tongue out, dove into the pool. The creek made a bend there, the force of water had dug out a small swimming hole. It was a favorite bathing place for the family. This morning, the water was still cool, the way the girls liked it. John and Evie never used it until the sun was high, the water warm.

When Betsy's head reemerged from the water, Laura started her harangue again.

"Go get us our robes, Betsy!"

"Wait'll you see him. Gunn. He's big and strong and he kisses like fire."

"Don't talk that way!" Laura paused, suspicious. "What else did you do with him?"

"Everything," Betsy laughed, diving under again so that her sister had to live with her shock.

"Everything?" as Betsy's head bobbed up from the pool.

43

"Ummm. Everything."

"You little hussy!"

Betsy dog-paddled around in a little circle. She paddled to a shallow part, stood up in the water. She began bouncing her breasts with her hands, then began tweaking her nipples. Laura stared at her in indignation.

"Don't do that, Betsy!"

"You do it. All the time! I've *seen* you!"

Laura's face flushed a deep crimson.

"And you play with yourself at night, under the covers!" Betsy's eyes flashed mischievously.

"Betsy! Stop talking like that!"

"It's so! What are you so mad about? I do the same thing. Mamma does too . . ."

Laura waded into the water, angry. She grabbed her sister's hair, jerked it.

Betsy screamed.

Laura slapped her.

Betsy tried to get away. Laura tightened her grip on Betsy's hair, started to drag her toward shore. Betsy fought, pummeling Laura with tiny fists. The water thrashed as they struggled. Laura shoved Betsy's face under. Betsy grabbed for her sister's breasts with both hands. She touched the full globes, clawed them. Laura released her grip on Betsy's hair. Betsy rose up out of the water, gasping for air. Her hands slid from Laura's breasts, down her legs. She grasped them tightly, dug in her fingernails.

Laura fell backwards.

Betsy slithered over her, trying to pin her underneath. Their bodies touched, writhed.

Laura spluttered to the surface, wild-eyed. She looked for Betsy.

Betsy swam underneath her, between her legs. She grabbed her pubic hairs, pulled them.

Laura screeched loudly.

"You little bitch!" she exclaimed.

"Laura!"

Evie stood on the bank, towels and robes folded over her arm.

Laura froze.

Betsy, hearing her mother's voice, poked her head out of the water.

"What are you two girls doing?"

"Betsy hurt me," said Laura, near tears. "She was fooling around with that man Gunn last night."

"Shut up, Laura!" exclaimed Betsy. "You—you liar!"

"Betsy," said her mother quietly, "get out of the pool. Dry yourself off and put on this robe. Laura, there's no excuse for this. You both are too old to fight like wildcats. I could hear you clear up to the house."

Both girls came up, naked, dripping water. Their mother looked at them, handed them towels.

"I'll talk to you later, Betsy," said her mother. "It's time we did."

She watched her daughters towel themselves dry and something ached in her breasts. They looked so young and alive. She envied them. She felt as young as they, inside, but something was withering away deep in her heart. Once she had been like they, and now they made her feel very old.

"Hurry," she said, and wondered if she was talking to them or to herself.

She had seen Gunn, too, and he was not much younger than she. In his late twenties. Handsome, in a rough, crude way. She had looked at his lips and at his tight trousers, the bulge at his crotch. A heat had arisen in her and she had crept away from the window, ashamed. Now, looking at her naked daughter, Betsy, she wondered if Gunn had slept with

45

her. There was no way to tell. But there was something going on. Maybe only a desire. But she knew what that could lead to. She knew. John had been that way, once. Young, virile, handsome. Wicked.

Like Gunn.

Suddenly, she wondered if she mustn't say something to her husband, ask him to fire the stranger.

And just as suddenly, she knew she wouldn't.

"Hurry up," she said again, and the girls both looked at her strangely.

CHAPTER FIVE

Gunn spent the day listening to the drovers, skinners, shooters, the cook, and Curly Cow Charlie talk about running buff. There were two wagons John Masters had ordered from St. Joseph, one drawn by twelve mules for hauling hides to market, a smaller, six-mule rig for carrying camp gear. Each wagon was sturdy, had iron wheels with treads nine inches wide and boxes made from one-eighth inch steel.

"Them two wagons cost about one thousand dollars," said Bucky, proudly. "John gets the best gear."

He met the cook, a black man, named Owl-Eye Harry. Harry had big eyes and the whites made him look even blacker. He was a good-natured man, and, as Gunn found out at lunch, a fair cook. The camp tender was a young man named Elmo, who was like a mascot. The buff runners had adopted him. He had kinky red hair, freckles, said he was eighteen, but looked about twelve. There was a French-Canadian skinner named Kerouac, but no one could pronounce his name. They called him Jack, although Gunn thought his name was Petit Jacques or Beau Jacques. He spoke French so fast when asked his name, and laughed so much, Gunn could barely make it out. He called him Jack and that was all right with him. He was a dark-haired man, lean-featured, who wrote poetry all the time and sharpened his blade. He seemed at home with himself, with the world, although there was a far-away look in his eyes as if he longed for Canada or worlds beyond.

"You and John will do most of the killing," Charlie told him. "You don't need many good shooters. He's a crack shot. If he tells you a certain buff to shoot, make sure you shoot that one. He knows."

Gunn listened, didn't say much. Jed, who was to be a skinner, spent most of his time with Kerouac, talking about knives, skinning, the challenge of taking off a buffalo hide without ruining it.

"You get to skinnin' a buff's winter coat," said Bucky to Jed, "you got to put up with grit. Hide's plumb full of it. Take the edge right off your best ol' knife. We was up the Santa Fe trail once't and it was 'bout ten above zero when we got into this herd. Skinners cursin' at the tallow when they went to sharpen their knives. Stiff on the blade, glazed the whetstones and steels, so they had to build a fire to soften that tallow."

"By gar," said Kerouac, "you tell it right, Bucky. And dose green buffalo hides weigh two hundred, three hundred pounds. You get big muscles, Jed Randall, by gar."

Jed laughed, joined by the others.

"These boys have hunted the good buffalo rivers,"

Curly Cow Charlie told Gunn. "The drainages is where the buff run. We all, at one time or another, hunted the Red, the Canadian, Cimarron, Arkansas, Solomon, Platte, Niobrara and the Republican."

"Where do you sell the hides?"

"Nearest market, generally. Denver, Dodge City, Laramie City, whatever town's handiest. You shoot and skin until the big wagon's plumb full. Maybe thirty-five bales. Ten hides to a bale. Runs around nine thousand pounds."

Gunn let out a low whistle of surprise.

"Oh, you won't get rich," said Danvers. "Poverty wages, mostly. But it's an adventure and you got your grub. Ain't no better meat than buff. I reckon I've earned, all tolled and tallied, an average of a hundred dollars a month. Better'n most cowhands do, at that."

"I've heard that shooting buffalo from a stand is about as exciting as killing beeves in a slaughterhouse."

Danvers laughed.

"Oh, that part of it is just dull work, friend. It ain't the killing of buff that's fun, it's the hunting of them. They's still millions left, but they're scattered all over hell and gone. You hunt these southern buffalo grounds, you got the Apaches and Comanches to look out for. Drives 'em plumb loco to see white man shootin' buff. Up north, you got the Sioux, Blackfeet and Cheyenne raggin' your ass. You get used to it. Keep your ears sharp. You hear a rifle shot, pay real close attention to it. If it's a distant heavy thud sound, probably a big-bore buffalo gun. If it's the sharp crack of a small caliber, most likely an Injun."

"You've still got your hair," Gunn observed.

"I been lucky."

Gunn took a lot of kidding about going to supper

48

with the boss. He took it good-naturedly. He was rested after a good nap, a bath in the creek. Bucky lent him a razor and he scraped his face smooth. He thought of slicking back his hair, but decided against it. It was ragged at the edges, but clean. When the dinner bell clanged, he left the bunkhouse, boots polished, clothes brushed.

John Masters answered Gunn's knock.

"Come in," he said, taking his pipe from his teeth. "How about a drink of whiskey?"

"Obliged."

Gunn heard the women's voices in the next rom, the clatter of dishes. He could smell the aroma of food cooking. The Masters' livingroom was not large, the furnishings spare. But it was a man's room. A rifle over the fireplace mantle, pistols, flintlocks, on the walls, dried flowers in vases. It looked like a place that could be closed up, locked and left for long periods of time. The furniture was handmade. Buffalo rug on the floor, the couch made of buffalo hide, a mounted head on one wall, massive.

Masters poured two glasses of whiskey, four fingers in each. He handed Gunn a glass.

"I drink it neat," said John.

"Fine."

"Here's to a good hunt." Masters clinked his glass against Gunn's.

Both men sipped their drinks, then John waved Gunn to the divan while he sat in the master chair, also made of buffalo hide. Smoke from his pipe curled in the air. Lamps threw a friendly warm glow over the room. It was not chill, but logs were stacked against the hearth and there were signs the fireplace had been used recently.

Masters wasted no time in getting to the point.

"You stood up to Wayne Simons. He won't forget it.

Worse, neither will his pa nor his brothers. Claude is mean, but he's not a hothead. He's tough as a keg of nails. His sons, though, are about as wild as they come. Quick on the trigger."

"I heard that."

"I'm grateful you stood up for Betsy. I suppose she would have come to no harm. But I'd have had to take Elmer Keener down a peg for humiliating her."

"He was drunk."

Masters looked at Gunn with narrowing eyes. He stirred the bowl of his pipe, tamped it with a nail.

"You the Gunn I heard about up in Wyoming? Worked for the Association."

"Maybe. I did some work up there."

"Scared hell out of a lot of owlhoots. I heard about that business over in Palomas too. With Torreon. That you?"

Gunn nodded.

"You're not a gunslinger." It was a flat statement.

"No."

"But you hired out your gun in Wyoming."

"Not exactly. I raised cattle. The rustling was pretty wide open. I helped out some friends."

"Palomas, too."

"Look, Mister Masters, John . . . I don't see what you're getting at. If I have a reputation it's not my doing. I keep to myself, I'm not wanted by any law, and I thought you hired me on as a hunter. If there's any problem, I'll just ride on. I probably wouldn't like killing buffalo much anyway."

Masters laughed low in his throat.

"I guess I was putting you on the skillet some, Gunn. I like a man with mettle. We ride through a lot of country. See people. Some come out to watch us hunt, or count our hides. They stay, have some beans and bacon with us, a cup of coffee. Stories are told around the campfire. I was just curious to see if you were the same man some of these stories were about."

"I could be. I don't know."

John's face flushed warmly. He beamed at Gunn.

"Some of them would curl your hair."

"I reckon." Gunn sipped the rest of his drink. The two men sat silently for a while.

"John!" called Evie. "Bring our visitor to table."

"Just leave your glass. The womenfolks will clean up after us. Come on and break bread with us, Gunn. I need you."

"Eh?"

"Why, I'm outnumbered most of the time. You ever try to get a word in edgewise with three women talking at once?"

Gunn laughed. He liked this big gruff man. Masters was blunt, seemed genuine. They walked into the dining room which was part of the kitchen. There were rooms off the hallway, another hall angling off the kitchen. The house was bigger than it looked, sprawling, as if rooms had been added as the family had grown.

Evie Masters took Gunn's hand, introduced him to her daugher, Laura.

"Gunn, I believe you know my daughter, Betsy."

"Betsy," he said. But Laura caught his eye. Her name was so close to his wife's and she was such a contrast to Betsy. He noticed, too, that Evie seemed to be watching him. Like a hawk.

Laura met his gaze, her eyes sparkling as if she knew a secret. From that look, Gunn knew that Betsy had probably said too much. He wondered, as he sat down, if Evie Masters knew the truth. It would be difficult, he surmised, to get much past the woman. And, she was handsome, youthful in appearance, clear of face and eye, as beautiful in her way as her beautiful daughters.

Supper was rabbit stew and venison cutlets, potatoes, gravy, biscuits, hot coffee, turnips, slabs of chocolate for dessert. Mexican chocolate: rich, sweet, dark, narcotic.

Evie, he learned, was smart, self-taught. She had married John Masters when she was quite young, but she had not neglected her education. Yet, she had no pretenses. She didn't aspire to be a great woman, but she was, nevertheless. She had a quiet charm, an observant and considerate nature. She was also very prideful of her daughters, concerned that they grow up knowing what was right even if they did not follow her precepts.

"I believe a child should follow a parent's example, don't you, Mister Gunn?"

"It's just Gunn, ma'am, and I reckon a child will follow any example that suits 'em."

That was the first time he heard Mrs. Mastes laugh. But it was a harsh laugh, edged with a mother's suspicion. All through the meal Betsy kept making eyes at him, trying to establish an intimacy that he didn't want revealed. He wanted, in fact, to kick her under the table. But Laura was no less solicitous of his attentions. She flirted, batting her big eyes at him until he felt skewered. John Masters looked at him, now and then, with sympathy. It didn't help.

"Are you looking forward to the expedition, Gunn?" Laura asked, over the chocolate.

"I—I'm hoping to learn something new," he said awkwardly.

"We have fine times," said Laura. "Especially at night."

Gunn didn't know what to say. He said nothing.

"Oh yes," said Betsy, "at night, we sing songs and dance, try to sneak away from Mamma."

"Betsy!" reprimanded Evie, her face blushing with color. "Mind your tongue!"

"Oh, Mamma, I was just kidding."

John Masters lit his pipe, leaned back in his chair. He seemed to be enjoying Gunn's discomfort.

"The girls are a little headstrong, but Evie keeps 'em in check. She remembers all too well how I wooed her."

Masters winked. Evie blushed again.

Gunn squirmed in his chair, wanting to roll a cigarette.

"Betsy," John said, as if reading Gunn's mind, "fetch us some of that good *aguardiente* we got from Jose. Prime stuff, Gunn. Want to smoke? Evie doesn't mind it in the house, unlike most women."

"A man should smoke in his own home if he wants to," said Evie primly.

"Laura batted her eyes at Gunn while Betsy was gone. Her breasts seemed to swell every time he looked at her. She was hard to ignore.

Evie took Betsy's absence as an opportunity to say what was on her mind.

"Forgive me for being blunt, Gunn," she said, "but I'd like to talk to you privately before you leave this evening. John, don't interfere. I'll speak my piece and then the air will be cleared."

Masters nodded, puffing on his pipe.

"Whatever you say, Mrs. Masters," said Gunn.

"You can call me Evie. We'll be living in close harmony on the hunt. We don't put ourselves above any of the men."

"I see," said Gunn, but he was already wary of Evie Masters. She was a smart woman. Tough. Beautiful as sin. She saw a great deal, he knew. He was not looking forward to their private talk.

Betsy returned with the brandy, poured some in

small earthen cups. Laura filled the water glasses. The women all wore prim dresses, but they were startlingly beautiful.

"We'll plan to get started day after tomorrow," said John. "You and Jed go into town tomorrow, get your things ready. I'll provide the rifles, ammunition. You'll bring your own horses, bedrolls."

"Fine," said Gunn.

The brandy was indeed fine. It tasted of musty grapes and ancient vinyards. It had an edge to it. Gunn rolled a cigarette while those at the table watched him in silence. He did it quickly, expertly, fished a sulphur match out of his vest, struck it on his boot heel. The tobacco flared into flame.

"Girls," said John, "would you clear up the supper dishes? I'm going to turn in. Evie. I'll say goodnight now."

John got up, kissed his wife, squeezed her. It was an appealing demonstration of honest affection. Gunn was impressed. Laura cleared his plates away. He wondered if she brushed a breast against his arm deliberately. He felt a tug at his loins, looked up at her quickly. She smiled, scurried away. But Evie's eyes were on him and he knew that she had noticed. Yet there was no accusation in her eyes, no censure. Only a look that was open and knowing. It gave him a sudden chill.

Gunn waited on the porch, a cigarette glowing in his fingers. Stars winked in the deep blue sky, a half-moon sailed like a shining ship high above thin fingers of clouds. He heard the door slam, saw Evie's silhouette against the orange glow of lamplight.

He drew on his cigarette, held the smoke for a moment, savoring it. He let it out in a grey plume that disappeared in the darkness. He put out the glowing butt against his bootheel, threw the dead quirly over the porch.

She came close, stood next to him. He saw part of her face limned in the light. Part of it was in shadow. She breathed, stared at him as if scanning his features.

"I wanted to talk to you about my daughters."

"Why?"

"Don't be impertinent, please. I want to keep my voice down so that they don't hear me. And I don't want to disturb my husband."

"Supper was fine. I didn't know there was a catch to it."

"There wasn't. Until I saw Betsy looking at you. And Laura."

"I didn't encourage it."

"I know. But I'm not stupid, Gunn. You may have already had something to do with Betsy. She was in town last night. There was time. Opportunity. She's impulsive, wild. I can't change her. But Laura is refined, a lady. I warn you. Keep away from her or I'll make life miserable for you."

Gunn said nothing. His breathing was even.

"I mean it, Gunn. If John catches you with Laura on this expedition, he'd give you a choice. Marry her or die."

"Laura's over twenty-one. She may be a lady, as you say, but that doesn't mean she isn't human."

"What do you mean by that?"

"I mean," said Gunn, "that ladies make the same mistakes as men sometimes. I won't chase her, Mrs. Masters, but I don't want you sneaking up on me either."

"As long as we understand each other."

"I think we do, ma'am. Please tell the girls thanks for the hospitality. You too."

He started to move, but her hand shot out, touched

his arm. He felt the pressure on his elbow.

"Gunn . . . don't keep calling me Mrs. Masters . . . call me Evie."

"Evie . . ."

He heard her breath suck in. He thought she was going to say more, but she released her grip on his arm.

Gunn's boots rang hollow on the porch steps. He walked toward the bunkhouse. At the corner of the house, he turned, looked back toward the porch.

Evie was still standing there, a dark form in shadow.

He could have sworn she was waving to him.

CHAPTER SIX

Gunn and Randall left the Masters place before sun up. Gunn had no wish to spend another idle day there—especially after his talk with Evie Masters the night before. They said goodbye to Charlie, said they would wait for the wagons to come for their gear. Both he and Jed had a lot of things to buy that they would need on the expedition, things they would not carry on horseback.

"Steer clear of the Simons bunch," whispered Charlie, half-asleep.

"We'll do our best," said Gunn.

They were checked back into the hotel before noon, had most of their shopping done by suppertime. They bought buckskins, spare ammunition, knives, extra tack, canteens, good blankets, warm coats. They put the bundles in their rooms, cleaned up.

56

"Let's get a drink," said Jed. "All that running around tuckered me out.'

"Maybe we ought to get a bottle, drink in our rooms."

"You afraid you might run into Simons?"

"No use lookin' for trouble."

"Hell, they probably forgot all about it."

"Yeah," said Gunn, but he wasn't convinced.

"Hotel bar?"

"Good enough. I don't think Simons or his bunch hangs out there. Too tame."

Gunn couldn't have been more wrong.

The hotel bar was crowded with roughnecks. And women. Whiskey was flowing freely. Men in buckskins were on a roaring drunk. There was laughter, talk, the clink of glasses.

"Did you hear about the fire?" someone asked Randall.

"Nope. What fire?"

"Saloon across the street. The Red Dog. Some boys got drunk, started shooting up the place. Lamp oil caught fire. They all come over here."

"Anybody hurt?"

"Who could get hurt? I told you we was all drunk."

Randall laughed. Gunn frowned. He kept looking for Wayne Simons, but didn't see him. Elmer Keener, either. He and Jed shoved their way to the bar. A woman sidled up to Gunn, winked at him. She was young, wore heavy makeup. He ignored her, followed in Randall's wake as a path opened to the bar.

"A couple of whiskies!" called out Jed. "better bring the bottle."

Two seathing bartenders were trying to keep up with the overflow crowd. Gunn wondered what they were all doing there.

"The wagons are coming!" someone yelled, and

more than half the crowd pushed and bulled their way to the front door. A hush came over the saloon.

"What's going on?" Gunn asked a man next to him.

"Simons. Got his wagons in from St. Louis. He's going to try and beat Masters to the buffalo grounds this year."

"I didn't think they hunted the same places."

"Hell, they go where the buff are. Whoever's there first, has it best."

That made sense to Gunn, but now he wondered why the·competition was so fierce. Masters seemed to relish beating Simons to the hunt and now it seemed Simons had the same idea. Outside, there was noise and loud talk, some cheering. A few men drifted back in, but not before Gunn and Randall found a table where they could drink their whiskies without being jostled.

Gunn saw a woman come into the saloon through the lobby. She walked to the bar, leaned over, whispered something to the bartender. He shook his head. She scowled, then started to sit at a table alone. She saw Gun looking at her, came over.

"I—I don't want to sit alone. Do you mind if I sit with you? I'm waiting for someone."

Gunn and Randall scraped chairs. The woman was young, pretty, with a heart-shaped face, hazel eyes, auburn hair. She appeared to be nervous.

Gunn pulled a chair out for her, helped her sit down.

"You want a drink?"

"No thanks. I really shouldn't be here. Elmer said he'd pick me up an hour ago, but I've been waiting in my room all day."

"Elmer?" Gunn and Randall exchanged looks.

"Elmer Keener. He's a drover for Claude Simons."

"Oh," said Gunn. "Well, I think the wagons just got

in. He's probably outside."

Again Gunn looked at Randall. Jed shrugged. Gunn was trying to match up this woman with Elmer Keener. It didn't make sense.

"Uh, you could find him outside," Randall suggested again. As if he could already smell trouble.

"Elmer wouldn't want me to do that. I know him. If he just got in, he'll come in here first. He—he drinks some."

Jed's eyes rolled. Gunn had to turn away to keep from laughing out loud.

"Look," said Gunn. "It's all right if you sit with us, but I had some trouble with Keener. If he saw you with me he might get riled."

She looked at Gunn with a blank expression on her face.

"Elmer?"

"I believe that was his name. If you're his woman, there could be a heap of trouble. I mean you no harm, nor him neither. Jed, maybe we'd better get to that supper."

Gunn started to rise, but at that moment a bunch of men came through the street doors.

The woman started to say something, but her gaze drifted to the men heading toward the bar. One of them saw her, stopped. He stared at her, then glared at Gunn standing over her.

"Hold it, boys," he said loudly. "We got a situation here."

Everyone in the saloon froze.

The man who spoke was stocky, blond, with a pinched face, pug nose. He wore thin leather gloves, a pair of pistols turned butt-out from his holsters. He was about twenty-five or thirty.

"Mister, you crowdin' the wrong range," said the blond man.

"Are you speaking to me?" Gunn asked quietly.

Another man in the group said something to the blond man.

"He's the one what went out to Masters."

"Yeah," said the two-gun man, "I'm talkin' to you, mister. Emmy Lou, what you doin' with riff-raff what works for Masters?"

The woman, stunned, looked at Gunn, then back to the man who had spoken to her. She seemed confused. She started to cry.

Gunn stepped away from the table.

"You're pretty quick with words," he said.

The man who had spoken before, looked at Gunn, then at Randall.

"Where's Curly Cow Charlie?" he asked.

"None of your business," said Gunn.

"We want to know if Masters is putting his outfit together."

"You'll have to ask him that."

"We think you know, mister. We seen you riding that way with Danvers."

"Who's asking?"

The man cocked a thumb toward the blond man, stepping back into the bunch.

"Kurt Simons, that's who!"

A warning flashed in Gunn's brain. Kurt Simons was Wayne's brother. Here was the trouble he was trying to avoid. He didn't know who the other men were. Didn't know if they knew him. He could feel their eyes on him. The woman in the chair was frightened. All this was beyond her ken. She was trapped in the middle of something she didn't understand.

A chair scraped.

Randall stood up.

"Look," said Jed. "We were having a drink. This

woman come up and asked to sit down and . . ."

"That's a damned lie!" snapped the blond man. "Emmy Lou! You tell 'em plain! You're supposed to be waiting in your room for Elmer."

"Why yes, but I . . ."

"Hell, I know that man, Kurt," said a man in the bunch. "He's the one what buffaloed your brother Wayne. His name's Gunn . . ."

Kurt Simons turned to stone.

His face hardened. His arms turned rigid. Frozen anger radiated from his face, his stance.

"You Gunn?"

"Well, now, you're full of questions, Simons. If it matters, my name is Gunn."

"Damn your hide. You roughed up my brother and a friend of mine."

Gunn watched Simons and the other men. Maybe some of them remembered his shooting demonstration. But he and Jed were outnumbered. Worse, the girl was there. Right smack in the middle.

"You claim one as kin, the other as friend? Well, Simons, they were bulldogging a young lady and just got their fingers slapped was all. You want to make something more of it. Just step outside and we'll settle it."

The murmurs died down.

The challenge was laid out.

Kurt Simons ran a tongue over dry lips.

He thought of his brother, Wayne, what he had told him. "He was fast, Kurt. You never saw a man draw so fast." He thought of what the others had said about Gunn's pistolwork. The stunned looks on their faces. The awe in their voices when they spoke about the incident. He looked into Gunn's cold grey eyes and something inside his belly started to squirm, turn cold.

The men around him started to edge away.

61

"Not now, Gunn," said Kurt Simons. "I got work to do."

"Then get to it," snapped Gunn.

"Come on, boys, let's get out of here. Emmy Lou, you comin'? Elmer's goin' to want to see you."

"Yes—I—" she stammered, rising to her feet. She threw a pleading look back at Gunn. Simons and his bunch stalked to the door. He waited until Emmy Lou and the others filed out, then turned to Gunn for one last sally.

"If you ride with Masters, Gunn, you'll be sorry. Masters ain't comin' back from this one!"

Gunn took a step toward Simons, who wheeled and strode through the door. Jed put his arm out, staying his friend.

"Let him go. He's just a loudmouth."

"Yeah, Jed, he is that," said Gunn thoughtfully. "But I think he meant what he said."

Gunn stood at his door, stuck the key in the lock. Jed was still downstairs, having some brandy before going to his room. They had eaten a quiet meal two streets away at a small café where no one seemed to care about buff runners.

"Pssst!"

Gunn froze.

"Pssst! Mister Gunn!"

Gunn looked down the hallway. The candles in their brass containers flickered, showing barely enough light to see.

The voice was a woman's, but Gunn did not recognize it.

He stepped away from his door.

At the end of the hall, he saw a hand waving.

"Ma'am?"

"Please! Come! I want to talk to you."

Suspicious, Gunn walked toward the voice, his right hand drifting close to his Colt. There was something familiar about the voice, but the whisper distorted the words, covered up the woman's identity.

"Who are you?"

"Emmy Lou! Hurry!"

Emmy Lou? Then he remembered. The woman in the hotel saloon. He had almost forgotten about her. He wondered what she was doing up at such an hour, calling his name. Could he be walking into something? Was Elmer Keener down there with her, waiting to jump him?

He saw a thin sliver of light fall across the flooring. The sliver widened as he came closer, an orange band that splashed on the floor and wall as she opened the door for him.

"Quick! Inside!" Her voice was a loud whisper, her tone anxious.

"Are you alone?" he asked. "I don't want to step into something."

"Yes. I—I'm alone."

He came upon her, but she turned her head away quickly. Her hand gestured for him to come inside. He stepped through the door, his eyes scanning the room. He didn't want any surprises. No one was there. The door slammed. He heard the key turn in the lock, a thin, metallic sound like a spur hitting a cinch-ring.

The bed was rumpled, but the bedcovers not pulled down. A leather suitcase stood against the dresser, not fully closed, tongues and ears of clothing sticking out at the top and sides. A lamp burned on the dresser. Another one lit the table at bedside. A large carpetbag lay on the floor, its maw open, vacant, gaping.

She moved toward a chair, her back to him. She pulled it out, bade him sit down.

"Ma'am, unless you got a pretty good reason, I don't think it's such a good idea me being up in your room."

She turned to him, then, burst into tears. She bowed her head but not before he saw the swollen, bruised cheek, the thin line of blood across her chin.

"Jesus!"

"Please don't look at me—I—I just had to talk to you . . ."

He stepped up to her, tucked a finger under her chin. Tilted her face up so he could look at her. She closed her eyes as if to hide, but he held her firm. Someone had struck her in the jaw, on the cheek. Hard. He saw her arm, then. A blue-black bruise glistened ugly in the lampglow.

"Who did this to you?"

"E—Elmer . . . he—he . . . won't you please sit down? I've got to—my knees are shaking. I feel faint."

He helped her to a chair, took one for himself.

"Elmer beat you? Why? Is he *loco?*"

She sat in the chair, wringing her hands. She found a kerchief tucked in her waistband, dabbed at her eyes. She winced when she touched her bruised cheek. He saw now that the top buttons of her blouse were ripped off. Mounds of breasts pushed against the cloth as if struggling to pop free. She had trim ankles, a delicate neck.

"He—he got drunk. I tried to keep him from drinking, but he wouldn't listen. He dragged me into that Wild Cat Saloon. A filthy, stinking place. With all those bad-smelling men. He—got angry when Mister Simons told him that I was talking to you and your friend. He—he didn't understand. The whiskey . . ."

"A man doesn't have the right to strike a woman . . . shame you in public . . ."

64

"He—he didn't strike me there. Here. He—he came up, closed the door and started hitting me. He didn't know what he was doing. He was so drunk . . ."

"That's no excuse."

"No. I suppose not."

"Is he coming back?"

"No."

Gunn looked around the room again, curious. There was no sign that a man stayed with her. Only feminine things. From the looks of the suitcase and carpetbag, she had not been there long. A few hours at most. There was writing paper and envelopes on the table near the bed, an ink well, a wooden pen.

"Are you sure?"

"He—he went off with the others. To drink more, I suppose. Then—he's leaving in the morning. I—I may never see him again. But that's not what I wanted to talk to you about. I—I wanted to warn you. About what I heard . . ."

"What's that?"

"Simons and the others—there as a lot of talk. I wanted to get away, to put my hands over my ears, but Elmer wouldn't let me go. Gunn, I don't know what happened, but I've never heard or felt such hatred all in one place like that. They—they're going to kill you! Murder!"

He saw that she was on the verge of hysteria. Her eyes welled with tears. Her lips quivered. Beyond the tears, he saw a random flash of fear. And, too, a genuine concern.

"Just drunk talk," he soothed. "I wouldn't pay much attention to barroom chatter."

"No—I know my brother. He—he's unpredictable. Dangerous. He—that's why he left home. We live in Missouri. Did. He shot a boy, ran away. Pa died of grief two years ago. Ma died three months ago. I came here to tell him, give him his share of the money. I had to sell everything. People. They still remember Elmer shooting that boy. They wanted to take it out on me."

"Wait a minute," said Gunn. "Is Elmer . . ."

"He's my brother," she sobbed. "But I don't even know him anymore."

CHAPTER SEVEN

Gunn sat there, stunned.

"Your brother?"

"Why, yes. I thought you knew. I'm Emmy Lou Keener."

"Christ."

"You shouldn't swear. Blaspheme like that."

"Sorry. I just didn't know. I thought . . ."

Realization dawned on her.

"Did you think that Elmer was my husband?"

He looked at her closely. But he had not looked at Elmer long enough to recall his features. He had gotten it all wrong. Now it all made sense. He tried to picture Elmer's face, but he had been drunk. He was young, that was all he knew.

"I reckon I did."

"We're twins. Oh, I know we don't look much alike. Not identical twins. We were just born at the same time. Emmy Lou and Elmer Lou. Silly names."

"No, not silly."

"Back in Hollister, the kids used to tease us. I guess Elmer couldn't take it. He grew up with a chip on his shoulder. He was seventeen when he shot that boy.

They were swimming in Turkey Creek, shooting pistols. Elmer's hair was long that summer. Jerry Yocum started teasing Elmer. The other boys picked it up. Elmer just lost his temper. He told Jerry to quit. Jerry laughed. Elmer shot him. He died the next day. Elmer packed his things, stole a canoe, floated down the White River into Arkansas. I guess he fell in with bad companions. We would get cards every so often. I knew he was here in San Antonio, but didn't know where to write him. I just got the stage out at St. Joe, came here, started asking questions about where I could find the buffalo hunters. I saw Elmer two days ago, met the Simons. I didn't tell him about Ma then. Yesterday I had to move from the hotel, and when I got back they told me he went to pick up the wagons from the drovers who brought them in from St. Louis."

Talking seemed to calm her down. The hysteria subsided, but tears streaked her face, made her hazel eyes shine in the light.

"Elmer didn't seem to care about Ma. I—I didn't tell him about the money. Not after I saw how much he was drinking, the rough bunch he was with. He—he's changed. I don't think he's sorry for shooting Jerry either. Maybe he was just looking for an excuse to kill him. What do you think?"

"I don't know," said Gunn quietly. "Look, you better get some sleep. I'm leaving in the morning. With Masters."

"Aren't you afraid of them? Simons and his brothers."

"I'll have to look out for them. They're hotheads. Braggarts. Too bad your brother is with them. I feel sorry for you."

"I—I'll be all right. It hurts so much."

He didn't know if she was talking about the bruises

or about the changes she had seen in her brother. Probably both. He got up to leave. She rose, too, started toward him. She moaned, winced with a sudden pain. Her eyes rolled in their sockets. She gave a gasp, crumpled. He rushed to grab her before she hit the floor.

He caught her just in time, bent under her weight, braced himself to keep from falling with her on top of him. He lifted her in his arms, saw her eyes roll and close. Her head fell backward limply. Her whole body was lifeless, almost weightless. He carried her to the bed, lay her atop the coverlet. Her dress slid up her leg clear to her thigh.

The bruises were deep. Big purple splotches where she had been kicked or struck. Gunn felt a wincing spasm of empathy. He sat down beside her, gently tapped her cheeks.

"Emmy Lou," he said, "wake up."

She moaned. He saw the pain contorting her features even thoug she seemed to be in a deep faint. She twisted on the bed, one of her hands reaching behind her. As if someone had stabbed her.

He wondered what to do. Obviously, Emmy Lou had been beaten up more than he had realized. The bruise on her thigh was ugly. He took her hand, held it. She moaned again. Her eyes did not open.

"Emmy Lou . . ."

He looked again at the ripped buttons. There were two more, still fastened. He loosened them, turned her over on her stomach. He peeled the top of her dress down, gasped when he saw the purplish splotches on her back, the yellowing edges. Without thinking, he stripped her dress off her body, leaving her in panties and halter. He removed her shoes. They thumped on the floor.

Gunn's eyes narrowed to hard glittering slits.

Her body was smeared with bruises where she had been battered by her drunken brother. He must have kicked her, smashed her with his fists. Senseless. Cruel. He felt a tug at his heart. No one should have to suffer like this. Certainly not a young pretty woman who was not even of age. The horror and the brutality of it reminded him of Laurie. She had been battered in much the same way, except that, in her case, bones had been broken. Nevertheless, he knew how painful such deep bruises could be. In places, he was sure, the bone had been struck. Long-term pain, for certain.

He searched through her suitcase, found a robe. He held her tenderly while he slipped her arms through the sleeves. He made her head comfortable on the pillow. He looked through her carpetbag and suitcase for some salve, balm. Nothing.

It was late. Likely he would have a hard time finding liniment or medicants to put on her bruises. Also, he didn't want to leave her alone.

Elmer might come back.

He tried again to rouse her. He sat in a chair by the bed, calling her name.

Maybe, he thought, she needed rest. She was breathing steadily, but her face was pale, clammy with sweat.

Gunn stretched his legs out, pushed his hat off his forehead and leaned back in the chair. He closed his eyes, dozing. He tried not to think of Emmy Lou's splotched body, the terrible bruises that marred her delicate flesh. Images of his wife, Laurie, flashed in his mind, intruded on his thoughts of the girl on the bed. A drowsiness came over him, calmed his brain, seeped into his consciousness. He would stay until she awakened, then leave. Check on her in the morning. Offer what help he could. He tried to remember Elmer, teasing Betsy Masters, tried to imagine his face before him, his neck. He wanted to smash his face, squeeze his neck until his face turned purple. Purple as the bruises on his sister's flesh . . .

A spiderweb brushed across his face.

Something soft touched his lips. He was aware of heat, a dampness. A delicate feather stroking his nose.

It was all tangled up in the dream, in the darkness of his mind. As if he had been gone for a long time and didn't know where he had been. Images drifted across the sky of his mind like prairie clouds, like cottonwoods along the Platte, buttes rising up from the stark red-orange New Mexico land. Like ghosts drifting down mountain trails, through the Black Hills, over the Rockies, into the Sierra Madres.

His eyes opened and it was dark.

Yet someone was there. Palpable. Touching him. He had the impression he was in a room. Some room. His boot heels rested on hardwood. A night breeze flowed through his hair. His hat had fallen off. Curtains fluxed at the windows in ghostly motion, the floor creaked.

"Gunn? Are you awake?"

He did not know that. Not for sure.

The voice was vaguely familiar. Husked. Masked. Scratching at his memory. Sensual in the dark. With the musk that went with it. A woman's musk, vaguely poignant, like sage or dried summer flowers. A scent that stirred his loins in some dark primitive way that was exciting.

"Yes," he said, trying to define his surroundings, straining to see the shape he sensed before him. Conscious now of nakedness. He reached out a hand, touched bare skin. An electric sensation shot up both arms. His crotch tugged at the strain as desire began turning a part of him to bone.

"Thank you. Thank you for staying . . ." Her voice was disembodied, floating from another dimension, crisply soft in his ears. He felt her face come close, lean toward him. He pulled back, involuntarily, wry because his mind was not clear. He did not know who she was, where he was.

Lips touched his. Gentle. Pressed gently against his. His hands flowed around bare hips and the strain on his trousers was great as his manhood hardened with blood crowding the big veins.

Arms slithered over his shoulders, onto his back. He felt a weight slide onto his lap. A naked weight. And it was like being tortured. His trousers blocked him from feeling her and yet he burned from the touch of her skin against the denim material. The chair rocked with their weight and her kiss swarmed over his lips, rich as steam, tasty as Mexican chocolate.

She began to squirm in his lap, rubbing her naked buttocks against his hardened cock.

"Gunn," she breathed. "I—I want you so much I can't stand it."

And then he knew.

"Emmy Lou . . . you're quite a surprise."

"I don't know what came over me. Seeing you asleep in the chair, knowing you had undressed me. I suddenly wanted you. I want you now."

"We'll never get to it this way. I've got ten pounds of clothes on me."

She stopped squirming.

"Will you? Promise?"

Emmy Lou had started something. It was too late to walk away from it. The buttons on his trousers were about to explode. Blood throbbed in his temples. His loins ached for her.

"I promise. Just give me a minute to skin out of these clothes."

71

He heard her pad toward the bed in the dark. He sat down, shucked his boots, slipped off his gunbelt. He skinned out of his pants, shirt. Still aroused, he started toward the bed when he heard a match scrape.

The match flared into flame. Emmy Lou touched it to the lamp as Gun strode to the bed. The wick caught fire, smoke curled up the chimney until she adjusted the wick.

She stared at him in open-mouthed awe.

"I didn't think you were so big . . ."

"You made me that way."

"It's like magic."

"Yes. Are you going to talk all night or make room for me in your bed?"

She slid away, waited for him.

Her body was curved, the hips flared perfectly. The nest between her legs glistened in the lamplight, damp from desire. He lay beside her, touched her breast. She stiffened.

"That hurt you?"

"No. No. It felt good. Just a twinge is all."

"I don't want to hurt you."

She opened her arms. He went into them in an effortless slide.

"You make me feel better already," she husked, opening her mouth, tantalizing him with a wriggle of her tongue.

He squeezed her breast. It was ripe, full, a yielding sponge. He taunted the nipple with his finger. It hardened into a rubbery mass. He kissed her relentlessly, moving his tongue against hers. His hand went to her other breast. She shoved it into his palm boldly. Her thighs wiggled against him. The tip of his cock smeared fluid along her leg, drenched the fine hairs of her thigh.

Her other nipple hardened into a nubbin. Small

bumps appeared within the circles of her aureoles as desire flooded her. He broke the kiss on her lips, attacked her breasts.

"Oh, yes, Gunn, do that," she breathed. "It's so sweet, makes me feel so good."

He laved her nipples, swirled his tongue over the bumps on her aureoles. She arched her back, reached out for his swollen staff. Her fingers wrapped around its throbbing bulk, squeezed.

Gunn felt electricity shoot up his spine.

"It's even bigger than before," she said. "Bigger than anything."

"Anything?"

"I—I mean, I never did this before. Just teased some. I always backed out at the last minute."

"You what?"

Gunn stopped mouthing her breasts.

"I'm a virgin, Gunn."

"Christ. Why did you have to pick this time to lose your virginity?"

"Don't be angry. I—I couldn't help myself. I've never felt such a strong attraction for a man before."

"Well, you might. And you might want to marry that man."

She grabbed him, pulled him close. His chest crushed her breasts, mashed them. She kissed his neck, behind her ears, peppered his shoulders with mock-savage bites.

"I don't care. Not now. Not tonight. Please, Gunn. I just want you. Now. As the first, not the last, necessarily. Just the first. Break me open. Put yourself inside me. Teach me."

She gasped, thrashing on the bed.

He felt himself being pulled down into a whirlpool from which there was no escape. She was wanton. Eager. Lusty. Yet, too, she was a purring kitten, a child full of hunger. He understood.

There was no going back now. No walking away.

Emmy Lou had spoken. The rules were hers, but he still didn't know why. Nor did it matter. His senses were scrambled, screaming. Her body was warm against his. Her flesh beckoned. He was a man and he was ready. Stone ready, his cock hard as rock.

"Spread your legs," he said softly, gruffly. "Brace yourself."

"Yes, oh, yes, Gunn. I'm ready."

Her legs widened. He looked down at her as he rose above her on stiffened arms. Down at her lampglow-softened face, her eyes, her lust-flushed face. Down at her smooth skin, her gently mounded belly, the dark thatch between her glowing legs, legs tawn in the light, legs pulsing with eagerness. A child, a woman. A mystery. He slaked his senses on her, then dipped his rock-mean cock down toward that small triangle of hair nestling between fleshy legs, toward the mask that hid so much pleasure in such a tiny space.

She gasped when he touched her. Her lips parted under the pressure of his bony thrust. A sigh escaped her. Her eyes widened, sparkled. He slid past the quivering lips of her sex, through the cleft, into the smoldering tunnel. Slid inside her slowly until she relaxed. Then bucked as a spine-rippling orgasm triggered a bucking spasm. She thrashed, her hips ramming upwards to smash against his own.

He held her tightly, listened to her mindless moans as the orgasm rippled, concatenated. Her eyes closed and her head thrashed from side to side on the pillow.

"Oh, oh, oh, yes, oh yes . . ." she babbled and he knew it was good. Would get better. He slid to the maidenly membrane, jabbed against it until he could stand it no longer. The crown of his cock was tender, tender as a fresh wound. But exquisitely pleasurable, in its sensation, as well. Tender pain.

"I don't want to hurt you," he said. "But it might hurt."

"I don't care, Gunn. I want it to—if it will make me remember you always. I'm—I'm in heaven or something. I didn't know it would be like this. So good, so wonderful."

He knew someone had to be first. Maybe it was important. He didn't know. It had been to Laurie. And to him, but his first was no good. He did not remember the woman's name. The whore's name. Nor her body, nor her innards. Not anything. He just remembered Laurie as the first good loving. The good loving. Would Emmy Lou think of him that way? He did not love her. He didn't know her. But she was pleasurable and womanly as any he had loved or bedded.

"I'm glad," he said, stroking her slowly, building up steam. She gasped, dug her fingers into his back. Bucked again as she climaxed. And again.

He battered her maidenhead gently, stretching it, weakening it. Felt it loosen.

"Brace yourself," he said.

"Yes, I'm ready. Tear it apart!" Her mouth opened and she looked up at him adoringly.

Gunn rammed hard and burst through the leathery hymen.

Emmy Lou spasmed with a galvanic thrashing that rattled her body as if she was a rag in the mouth of a savage hound. She cried out, wept, laughed, pounded his chest with tiny fists.

He burrowed deep, deeper still, until she held on to him, quivering with repeated orgasms. Held him deep inside her until he gushed his seed into her womb. Until a wave of peaceful lassitude washed over him and he fell, exhausted on her body.

He gave a part of himself up to her, became a boy again in her arms.

"Thank you, Gunn," she sighed, after moments, after weeks and years and centuries floated by. "I'm grateful. You made me feel like a real woman. You made me feel like living."

"You have a lot of life ahead of you."

"If you had not have come, I would have killed myself."

"No."

"Yes." She turned over and reached under the other pillow. She pulled out a small caliber gun, a pint bottle of whiskey. The pistol was a Smith & Wesson. The barrel gleamed in the light, the muzzle black as a cave. Light swam in the amber liquid of the bottle. "If you had not come, I was going to drink this and shoot myself."

Angry, he grabbed the pistol and bottle away from her.

"Don't," he gruffed, "don't ever. Life is too precious.'

She cringed from the terrible look on his face.

"I know," she said, almost whimpering. "I know now."

He hurled the bottle and pistol to the floor, held her tightly as she shuddered against him.

He would not leave her this night. Not all alone. Not to the darkness of her room, of her soul.

CHAPTER EIGHT

John Masters stood in the darkness, the coffee cup in his hand. His belly swarmed with moths, with the flutterings of winged creatures so familiar to him after all these years. The warm steam massaged his face, caressed his features as he looked for the first pale light to crease the eastern horizon. The porch creaked under his weight. He heard Evie and the girls move inside the house. The sounds were comforting.

In the dark shadow shapes of the land, he saw the buffalo, herds and bunches of them, rising from their nightbeds like broad shouldered giants with shaggy faces, mighty horns. Once, it was that way, he knew, and, like the Indian, he hoped it would be that way again. There was something about those big dumb beasts that got to a man, a hunter. He imagined, now, he could hear their rolling rumbling thunder across the plains, see their dark mass rolling across prairie, trampling the grasses, gouging out the dirt, racing toward some unknown destination as if driven by some mystical force.

The door opened; Evie came onto the porch, the bottle of whiskey in her hand.

"John? Are you all right?"

"Yes. Just anxious to get moving."

"I know." She came close to him, found the hot cup with her hand. The bottle was open. She poured some in the coffee, heard it hiss as the cold met the hot. "I'm excited too. It's always good to go out again, away from the town."

She didn't say it, but he heard her. Away from the empty house where he could no longer love her. To the emptiness of the prairie where she could be with men and her daughters and work from dawn till dusk to keep her mind off their troubles. She never said it, but her words were always there in his own mind. Shouting at him, accusing him, shaming him.

"I—I'm sorry, Evie," he stammered, and she held close to him. "I wish things were different between you and me."

"John Masters, you have never said 'sorry' to me before, and I don't want to hear you say it again. You're more of a man than any who lay claim to the title. I'm happy. Don't you know that?"

"You're not complete, Evie. I'm not complete. Not any more."

"Now, don't you start feeling sorry for yourself. You drink your coffee and the sun will come up like always and we'll ride out of here, find the buffalo."

He sighed. Evie was very wise. But she was lying. He knew that. She had been lying to him for a long time. To herself, probably, a lot longer.

"Did you give that new feller your regular talk?" Her heart quickened.

"You mean Gunn?" She knew who he meant.

"Yes. He might be a good man."

"I didn't talk to him like I usually do. He's different, somehow. He's not like the others."

"How do you mean?" His voice sounded faraway as if he was afraid to ask the question. As if he had turned his head away from her. But he was still looking out over the land, looking for the dawn to streak across the sky.

"He doesn't look at the girls. But they look at him. I think it's too late for Betsy."

"Umm."

"John, do you know what I'm saying?"

"Betsy was in town the other night. You think he seduced her?"

Evie stifled a dry laugh.

"The other way around. Gunn isn't like the others . . ."

"You said that."

"It's hard to explain. I don't think he's ever had to go after a girl. Or a woman. He's not exactly a handsome man, but he draws people to him. Laura would have done anything he asked when he was here. Betsy, too."

John was silent. She heard him nibble on his coffee, make gentle slurping sounds. She wished he would say something. Ask her what he wanted to ask. If she would do the same. The unspoken question hung on the air.

"Aren't you going to say anything, John?"

"What did you tell him?"

"There was nothing to tell him. He knew. I felt as if he had the upper hand. As if he knew more about Betsy and Laura than I do."

"Maybe he does, in a sense."

"John!"

"That man's a born leader. Yet he doesn't seem ambitious. There's iron in his backbone. He's the kind of man we need. Just keep the girls away from him, that's all."

She wanted to scream. *That's all?* Her insides were churning like a millrace. She fought to keep her emotions level. One part of her was urging caution and patience; while her instinct demanded that she tell John that Gunn should be left behind. But were her personal feelings important? Now? John was keyed-up, excited about the expedition. Did she have the right to question his selection of men? She had never doubted his judgment before. He had a sound set of values. He knew men. Those he didn't know he could usually bend to his will, either by setting an example or demonstrating his qualities of leadership.

Of course there was nothing outwardly wrong about Gunn. That was the trouble. His magnetism, a hidden energy, made her fearful. But of what? Of her daughters? No, not entirely. Or herself? Of her own feelings? Perhaps. Gunn seemed to have looked right through her. That was very unnerving to a woman. It was as if he did not respond to the eternal mystery, as if he could look behind a woman's mask and see the very essence of her. As if he could strip off her clothes and lay bare the lust that lurked in every woman's body.

Evie shuddered. That was the truth of the matter. Gunn made her feel vulnerable, naked.

"I'm sorry, John," she said feebly, "what did you say?"

A seam opened in the eastern sky. Light poured through the rent like pale cream, widening.

John finished his coffee in a single gulp.

"Huh? Oh, it doesn't matter. I'll get the boys. Time we packed up."

She took his cup, nodded numbly.

After he was gone, she remembered that he had looked right through her, never sensing the trembling inside her, the hurt that rose suddenly to the surface. Never seeing her as a woman, an aching, needful woman whose heart was about to burst.

But Gunn had seen that.

He had seen her clearly, deeply.

Claude Simons was part bear, part boar-hog, part bull. He was all man. He stood just under six feet tall, with a full beard, hirsute body half as wide as he was tall. He had no waist, but his torso was supported by legs as solid as oak stumps. His face was visible only at the cheeks and eyes. His chest swarmed with hair and part of it may have been his beard dripping onto it, and part of his beard may have been the mass of tangled curls that festooned past his broad yokes of shoulders. His eyes were rheumy, small, looked as if they strained to peer out through that mass of hair, while his nose was bobbed, the nostrils sprouting their own shoots of scraggly hairs. His sloping skull was hidden under a bandanna that crimped his hair down to keep it out of his small eyes. His wrists were as big as most men's calves. There was fat on him, but it was slabbed on thick and hard over big bones. When he walked in a room, the floor thundered. When he spoke, the walls rattled.

Claude Simons was plain big and plain mean.

"Get your lazy asses up!" he roared, kicking a bunk so hard the slats rattled.

Wayne Simons tumbled to the floor, groggy.

Kurt sat up, blinking like a disheveled owl.

Lefty peeked out from under a blanket. The room reeked of whiskey, tobacco, piss, rawhide and sweat.

"Jesus, pa, it ain't even daylight," said Lefty.

"You won't see daylight, you don't get crackin'," boomed his father. "We got work to do and we're damn well gonna break ass to get to it."

The boys got out of their bunks. The memory of stinging ears was still fresh in their minds. When they were small, their father boxed their ears when they disobeyed, or when they were slow. He would do worse, now, they knew. The three boys respected their father, but they were afraid of him too. Wayne, the youngest, was most afraid. His face still hurt where his father had slapped him after hearing of the incident in town with Gunn.

Lefty, the middle boy, was the least afraid. He had escaped the brunt of punishment during his growing-up years. Kurt, the oldest, had gotten more than his share of thrashings and was always blamed for the faults of the younger boys. Even now.

"Get 'em goin', Kurt. We got wagons to load. We're gonna beat Masters this time."

"Yeah, Pa," said Kurt, searching for an errant sock. The floor of the bunkhouse was strewn with chicken bones, dried-out beans, scraps of tortillas, empty bottles, clothes, cartridges, tacks. "Ouch!" Kurt hobbled on one foot trying to remove a large tack from his big toe.

Wayne and Lefty snickered.

"Whyn't you clean this place out, Wayne," said Kurt, extracting the tack. "Damn!"

"Hell, this ain't my mess."

"We ought to get a woman to come in," said Lefty. His name was Rupert, but no one dared call him that. He was a scrawny man in his early twenties with a finger missing from his right hand. That's why they called him "Lefty." He was right-handed, but every time some one saw his right hand with the middle-finger missing they made a joke about it. He didn't mind. He had lost the finger in a knife fight and cut the man's gut open who did it. The man lived, but he lived stooped-over as a perpetual reminder of Lefty's right hand.

"What woman would come in here?" asked Kurt, finding his dirty sock.

"A Mex, like the one what cooks for us," said Wayne, slipping into stiff denims.

"Pa says we got to pay fer her ourselfs," said Lefty. "Hell, I ain't gonna waste two dollars on a maid when I can get two bottles of whiskey for the same price."

Kurt guffawed and Wayne kicked an empty can of

peaches across the room. It clattered against the wall with an accusing clang.

The boys had been motherless ever since Wayne was born. She died giving birth to him, but nobody held any open resentment against him for her death. Kurt claimed she was a tired old woman anyway and too thin to bear children. Lefty said he didn't remember her much. Pa had raised them anyway, on buffler meat and wild rabbit.

"Seen Elmer?" asked Wayne, tugging on his boot.

"I seen him last night," said Lefty. "Drunker'n seven hundert dollars. Slapped his sis around, he said, and was crying in his tequila."

"Elmer's a prick," said Kurt, searching for a shirt in the bedclothes. "His sister's a mouse."

"He was plenty mad that you saw that Gunn feller with her," said Lefty, smoothing out the crease in his hat before putting it on. "Claimed he was going to put that jasper up to the wall."

"Shit," said Kurt. "Elmer couldn't shoot his way out of a sling-shot match."

"Yeah," said Wayne, anxious to pick on someone else for a change, "Gunn would shoot his ass off."

"You tell 'em, horseshit," said Lefty, "you've been on the trail."

Wayne grabbed a whiskey bottle and hurled it at his brother. It sailed out the window, thudded to the ground.

"Cut it short," said Kurt. "We ain't got time for no grab-butt here. But you brought up a fuckin' point, Wayne. That Gunn is a smart-ass sonofabitch. Pa wouldn't mind it none if we took the bastard out since he's thrown in with Masters."

"Yeah?" said Wayne.

"You serious?" Lefty asked.

"Dead serious. Besides that, Pa wanted me to talk

to you about an idea he had. But don't tell Elmer ner no one about this. Could mean your asses."

"Hell, Kurt, we ain't gonna flap our jaws, spill your beans and we'll lap at 'em." Lefty got his hat right, set it on his head.

Kurt smiled thinly, slipped on his shirt which had been stuffed inside his torn pillow, threw a leg up on the bed. He leaned on his knee, gestured with his hands as he spoke.

"Pa figgers to beat Masters out of the barn, head for the Cimarron. Now, along the way, we kind of linger back and . . ."

Jed Randall hung on the edge of death.

He wanted to die.

Men with mauls were smashing his head. Pygmies with darts wre hurling them from blowguns into his eyes. His eyes burned as if hot needles had been driven into them from in front and behind. The biggest longhorn steer in the world had a horn in his gut and was twisting it until every nerve was screaming.

Someone had shat in his mouth.

"Jed, you are a sorry sonofabuck," said Gunn, looking at his friend on the bed. "I swear, son, you must have drunk all the whiskey in San Antone last night."

Jed opened one eye, closed it quickly for fear of bleeding to death. He moaned and the moan caused him deep pain. A hatchet smashed into the back of his head. Lights danced in his skull.

Gunn nudged the naked man's bare foot with the toe of his boot.

"Time to rise and shine. Heap big buffalo hunt."

"Fuck you, Gunn!" The voice that came out of Jed's mouth was not his own. It belonged to a man who had been flayed alive, left buried in an anthill with honey smeared all over him. It was more of a croak than a human sound.

"Do you think we have time?" Gunn laughed.

"Jesus, Gunn. I'm dying. Will you do me a favor?"

"Shoot."

"Yeah. My pistol. Get it. Cock it. Hold it up to my temple. Squeeze the trigger. I'll be eternally grateful."

Gunn laughed, came around the edge of the bed. It had taken a lot of persuasion to get the clerk to let him in Jed's room. This, after pounding on the door for fifteeen minutes with no answer, save a few savage screams and animal-like moans. He had seldom seen Jed so hungover, but the sight was painful. It was shortly after dawn and time for them to get their gear ready. The wagons would be coming for them soon.

"I ought to do it."

"Please. I'm begging."

"You'll feel better once you get some coffee in your belly."

Jed groaned.

"No. I won't. I'm dying. Pure dying."

"How about if I just shoot one of your nuts off? Think that'd get you going?"

Gunn drew his pistol, cocked it.

That caught Jed's attention. He opened one eye again. Then the other.

"You wouldn't . . ."

"I might. I'm in a terrible hurry."

Jed sat up. This was not as easy as it sounds. First he braced himself with one arm on the bedpost, the other on the bed. As if holding it steady. He struggled to a sitting position, started to sag back down, then summoned up the remainder of his strength and held steady.

He looked at his naked body in bewilderment.

"Somebody robbed me! Stole all my clothes."

Gunn let the hammer down on his pistol, holstered it and bent over. He picked up a bundle of clothes, a wallet.

"Will these do?"

He threw them to Randall, who shied as if a stone had been hurled. The bundle landed in his lap.

He looked through the wallet. Shook it. It was empty.

"Robbed," he said quietly.

Gunn suppressed a laugh.

"How many whores did you bring up here?"

A light dawned in Jed's consciousness.

"Two."

"Americans?"

"Of course, Americans. Why?"

"Just checking. I didn't want to start no war with Mexico."

Jed saw that he was being ragged. He made a face at Gunn. This cost him a little more pain. He winced as if shot through with a dozen arrows.

"Come on, Jed," said Gunn, "we're going to hunt the mighty buffalo. I need a good skinner."

Jed winced again. "Don't say that word. I feel like I been skinned alive."

There was a bottle on the nightstand with about two fingers of whiskey left in it. Jed reached for it.

Gunn snatched the bottle away.

"Coffee. No whiskey until after you've skin . . ."

"Dammit, Gunn, I told you not to say that word."

The whoops and hollers outside the window made the two men start. Gunn walked over, pulled the curtain aside. The window looked down on Juniper Street. Men and mules, horses and wagons crowded the street. People were cheering. Gunn's face shadowed.

"What is it? Masters here already?" Jed tried to

stand, couldn't.

"No," said Gunn. "It's the other bunch. Simons. They're rolling and we're sitting here with our thumbs up our butts."

The teams strained at their traces. Leather creaked. Gunn looked down and saw Elmer Keener, Wayne Simons, Kurt Simons, others he didn't know. The only thing he could say was that Elmer looked far worse than Jed. Someone was holding him on the seat, another was passing him a bottle. Keener's hand shook as he took it, juggled it with the reins.

Gunn thought of Emmy Lou, sleeping in her room. If she was lucky, Elmer wouldn't come back.

CHAPTER NINE

The Masters outfit, although better organized, left San Antonio several hours behind the time Simons had departed. John Masters knew the trail ahead, knew its dangers. So did most of his men and the women in his household. When he learned that Claude Simons had left shortly after dawn, he decided to hold back.

"I don't want him to think we're doggin' his tracks," he told his men, "and we sure as hell aren't going to eat his dust. Let him go his own way, and we'll still find better pickin's."

His men cheered and he kept them busy double-checking all the supplies, bought two *ollas* of *tepache* to ladle out when the sun got high. It wasn't enough to get anyone drunk, but adequate to make everyone who drank it feel good. The brew, of beer and fruit, was cheap and mildly intoxicating. It was also refreshing and not a man-jack among them complained about the delay.

"Masters knows men," said Gunn to Randall, who had just recently begun speaking civilly to him again. "That is sure one hell of a trail we're takin' north."

"I wish he'd lay over another day," said Randall, still affected with a smattering of self-pity.

"Hell, you already lost all your money and probably got a dose of the clap to boot."

"True, Gunn, true. I just feel like I've been put together by a barber, that's all."

The wagons rolled at John Masters' signal. He rode ahead on a big-boned gelding. Gunn and Randall flanked the rear wagon. The women rode in the first covered wagon, behind them, the chuck wagon, then the supply wagon, another smaller wagon and two large hide wagons. Way behind, two Mexicans handled the small remuda.

The women rode in front so they would have to eat less dust. Gunn had scarcely caught a glimpse of them all morning. But that was all right. He would leave them alone, if they'd do the same. Once, though, he had caught Betsy trying to get his attention with her eyes. It was better to ignore her, because her mother was watching too. Laura never looked his way once, as far as he knew.

The Chisholm Trail was no longer a small cattle trail, nor a wagon road like the one Jesse Chisholm first laid out straight and level. After more than a million head of cattle had gouged it, wagons had rutted it, horses had trampled it, it was now a desolate stretch of eroded earth in the middle of hell. Sometimes the trail was from 200 to 400 yards wide. Erosion had undercut the trail in places to bring it below the level of the plains it crossed. Strewn along the trail were the bleached bones of cows killed by disease, stampedes, or bullets. Cows that couldn't keep up were shot. Calves, birthed along the drive, were often too weak to keep up the pace. These were dispatched efficiently.

Here, too, were the shallow graves of men who gave up their lives on the long brutal cattle drives, a drover drowned at a river crossing, a cowhand with a burst appendix, a settler killed by Indians. Men didn't count much on a drive. "Look out for the cows' feet and the horses' backs and let the cowhands and the cook take care of themselves," was the refrain repeated by every trail boss who moved a herd up the Chisholm.

Earl Pettibone was not the first victim of the Chisholm. Nor would he be the last.

Pettibone was twenty-one years old, was born and bred in Texas. He had hired on as a drover's helper, but had dreams of running buff. Today he rode the small wagon which carried extra tack, ropes, tents, stakes, anything that wouldn't be hurt too much if it rained. Alongside him, driving the two-horse team, was an older man, Lem Simpkins who had a wooden leg. Lem was a former skinner, but a slipped knife had cut an artery and the tourniquet had caused gangrene to form. He had lost the leg, but was glad to be alive.

As the Masters expedition crossed the Colorado, a rifle shot exploded the silence. A puff of smoke appeared among the cottonwood trees on the other side. The horses spooked. For a time, no one knew what had happened.

John Masters was in the middle of the ford, the covered wagon just behind him. The chuck wagon was upstream, slightly, fording well, and the other wagons were all in the water. On the south bank, Gunn and Randall waited, watching for any signs of trouble: current, slippage, soft sand under a wheel. Anything. Anything but gunfire.

"What was that?" asked Jed.

Gunn's eyes narrowed. He saw the small puff of white smoke in the trees on the north bank. Then, the smoke began to disintegrate and disappeared in the blue Texas sky, appearing only as wisps, like cobwebs torn down with a housewife's broom. He looked at the water for a tell-tale spout.

"I don't know. Someone shot a rifle. Big caliber."

"What's the range?"

"To here?"

"Maybe eight hundred yards. Six hundred easy."

"Couldn't be shootin' at us, could he?"

"Jed, I just don't know. One shot like that. Like a man had a target and then run off. Hit or miss."

"Jesus, Gunn, you give me the willies."

Gunn shoved Esquire into the river, spurring him down the bank. Randall, caught offguard, waited a few seconds before following.

The wagons reached the other shore. Gunn tried to follow the empty hide wagon between its ruts. Masters had picked a good ford. Sandbars broke up the flow of current, gave them footing. Islands that would not be there an hour from now, or ever again, likely. Esquire never got his belly wet, but by the time Gunn reached the shore the wagons had pulled up in a skirmish line, their backsides to the trees.

Gunn kicked the big sorrel, felt the horse's muscles contract under the saddle.

Masters was barking orders. Men were drawing rifles, looking in every direction, with fearful looks on their faces. Horses were snubbed down, held by taut reins.

"What's the trouble?" Gunn asked.

And then his stomach turned.

Lem Simpkins held the young man in his lap. Blood streamed from Earl Pettibone's throat, soaked onto Simpkins' sleeve.

Simpkins began rocking the dead boy like a baby, tears streaming down his face. His deep sobs made a terrible ripping sound in his throat.

"I didn't know," he wept. "I didn't know the boy was shot. All the way across I didn't know he was dying."

Evie came up, afoot, saw Simpkins holding the dead boy. She didn't wail, nor panic. Instead, she took a firm grip on Lem's arm, shook him.

"Lem, let me and the girls take care of Earl. Don't go blamin' yourself."

He looked at her with red-rimmed eyes. Betsy and Laura responded to their mother's urgent call, bringing a winding sheet with them. Some of the men helped get Earl out of the buckboard, carrying him to the covered wagon where Evie Masters could wash the blood off, prepare the youth for burial.

Gunn rode up to Masters who was deploying men in the skirmish line.

"Whoever shot that boy is long gone," Gunn said.

"How do you know?" asked Masters.

"One shot. Nothing after that. If you don't mind I'd like to check for tracks. I marked the place where I saw the smoke."

"You saw the shot? Heard it?"

Gunn nodded.

"Where?"

Gunn pointed.

"I'll get the men to . . ."

"No, Masters. Just me. I don't want anyone messing up the tracks. I can tell you one thing, though. It was a big caliber rifle. Probably a buffalo gun."

Whoever had shot Earl Pettibone had waited a long time for the opportunity.

The hoof prints were deep in the soft earth. Gunn ground-tied Esquire, went over the ground carefully.

Nothing distinctive about the hoofprints.

No empty hull from the rifle.

Only a feeling, at fist.

The man.

Sitting there on a horse. Waiting. He had steadied the rifle against a tree while on horseback. Good horse. Standing steady like that. There were slide marks where the horse had backed up at one point. Perhaps when the rifle had fired. But, short skids, the heels digging in deeper.

He found the place where the man had stepped down to pick up the empty shell. A careful man, perhaps. But brass was brass. Needed on the long ride where a man had to load his own. With a knife and primers, powder, ball. A rammer, vise. A hull would have helped.

Gunn let a curse flow over his lips like a wisp of a prayer.

He rode on out of the cottonwoods, following the tracks. Knowing he would learn nothing. Beyond the fact that the tracks led to the trail and the trail was a maze of tracks and ruts and meaningless sign.

And so it was.

They were burying Pettibone when Gunn got back.

"You find anything?" asked Masters.

Gunn shook his head.

"It was Simons," said Masters.

Gunn drew a breath, said nothing. The clods of dirt spattered on the winding sheet and the men and women stood around gazing at the emptiness of death in a shallow hole gouged out of mindless earth.

"Horse has a nubbed-off heel on its left rear shoe. Crooked enough so's I could spot it again."

"Good. You a tracker?"

"I've tracked some."

"From now on, you ride point. I don't want any more surprises."

Gunn's eyebrows went up.

"I know, I know. You could catch the next ball."

"I'm not worried about that so much. You goin' to be ridin' under a cloud the whole way."

"Could be, Gunn. Simons is scum, but I didn't think he'd go this far."

"Maybe it isn't just the buffalo's got him worried."

"I don't follow you."

"Pride. You've had your run-ins with him. I spanked one of his pups. Things like that get in a man's craw, they can eat him up."

Masters looked at Gunn carefully.

"Seems you know men."

"I'll take the point," said Gunn, wheeling Esquire away from the filled grave.

He rode up ahead, waved goodbye to Jed. Lem Simpkins put his hat back on, dried his eyes with a rein-chafed finger. Evie and the girls did not look up, but seemed to be mesmerized by the dirt mounding up over the shallow grave.

Gunn knew the tracks went north, when he picked them up again, over a rise, they were far apart. The horse was running, but it still left that tell-tale mark from its left rear shoe.

Masters made camp near Round Rock, above the Colorado River. There were signs that men had camped there before, but the Simons party had gone beyond that point. The horse Gunn had tracked had joined its mark with those of the wagons and other animals so that the spoor was a blurred pattern on the earth.

"Appreciate your riding point," Masters told him when he saw the wagons pull up and rode back. "Not much chance of an ambush for a ways."

"No, I reckon not."

"Pettibone was a good kid."

"He didn't need to die young."

"Wonder if you'd mind sleeping away from camp. You won't stand guard, but keep one eye open for me."

"Done."

Masters slapped him mildly on the back.

"Thanks."

The smell of beans and biscuits was powerful as dusk closed on the land. The horses and teams were hobbled, nibbled on patches of dried grass. Tomorrow they would get grain. The campfire threw cascades of sparks into the air. The smell of mesquite was strong, mixed with dried cowpies, pungent in the stillness of evening. The sun left a rowdy blaze on the purpling sky and the talk around the fire was gentle, subdued. Evie and her daughters were efficient, stirring the stew in the big iron pot, handling the long-handled skillets deftly.

Gunn ate with Jed and a group of men some distance away from where the Masters family sat. The coffee was strong enough to float a nail, the biscuits gluey enough to stick to a man's ribs after being dipped in the thick gravy.

Tin plates "washed" with sand, the horses blowing with rubbery nostrils, the plaintive sound of an harmonica, the rustle of cloth dresses, the yap-croon of coyotes—and night, fended off by the campfire, sparkling with stars—these were the sounds as the men lit pipes and rolled cigarettes after a filling meal.

Gunn and Randall sat with a few of the men—men they did not know very well. The harmonica stopped in mid-note and a silence settled on the group.

Two brothers, Gordie and Gee-Haw Winesap, looked at each other meaningfully. One nudged the other. They were not identical twins, but were born on the same day of the same mother, minutes apart. Gordie was prematurely gray, Gee-Haw had hair like the hide of a strawberry roan. Both boys were in their thirties, had a humorous cant to their smiles, twinkles in their merry blue eyes.

"Hey, Jed," said Gordie, "how much money you got in your pocket?"

Jed shrugged, looked bewildered. The question had caught him off-guard.

"Go on, tell us how much money you got," said Gee-Haw.

Randall fished in his pocket, drew out three blackened quarters.

"Six bits," he said earnestly.

Everyone laughed. Gunn didn't, but his senses perked as he sensed some tomfoolery going on.

"You broke?" asked Gordie.

Jed nodded dumbly.

Gordie pulled out a sheaf of bills, flapped them at Jed.

"Here's your money, Slim," he said.

"Huh?"

More laughter. Gunn laughed too.

"Go on, take it. It's yours."

Jed got up, stumbled over to Gordie. He took the bills gingerly in his hand. Stared at them while a dozen eyes glittered. He counted the bills. Once, twice. Then a third time.

"This is what I had in my wallet, I think. More or less."

"Yeah," said Gordie. "We fotched it for you."

"You caught the gals?"

Again the men laughed. Private laughs shared among conspirators.

Jed's face flushed in the firelight.

"You're makin' fun of me," he croaked.

"Yep," grinned Gee-Haw. "Gonna call you Six Bits from now on. Ever' man here has a nickname. Gordie and me, we got those gals to take your poke. You was drunker'n hell. We didn't mean no harm. Just wanted to see how hard your backbone was. Six bits. Haw! You come with us with only six bits to your name!"

"Not many'd do that," said Gordie. "You done rode one river with us, we figger you kin ride a couple more."

Jed staggered away, plumped down on the ground.

He stared again at the money, tried to remember what had happened. He shook his head in bewilderment.

"Look, son," said Curly Cow Charlie, "you just been accepted by this bunch. You got a nickname. Even John Masters has one."

"Yeah, what?" asked Randall.

"You'll find out when the time comes. You just keep your skinnin' knife sharp."

Gunn stood up, tossing away a cigarette.

"See you, Six Bits," he said, a smile curling his lips. "I got to get my bedroll and find a soft spot."

"Hey, Gunn, you don't have no nickname!" said Randall, as Gunn walked away from the firelight.

His words were swallowed up by the silence.

After Gunn left, Curly Cow Charlie drew some figures in the dirt with a stick. It was quiet and the men were all tired, sleepy. He seemed to have been thinking for a long time before he spoke.

"Man like that there," he said, "seldom gets nicknamed. Not that he ain't friendly, but he just carries something around with him. I seen it before. A kind of lonesome. You don't tag a man like that. You take him as he is and hope to God he don't turn on you."

In the covered wagon the women sighed and settled down to sleep.

A horse spraddled and peed on the dry ground. Steam hissed in the air.

Men went to their blankets, pulled off boots, tucking the tops in to safeguard against scorpions.

Nighthawks prowled the land with ghostly dollars on their wings, silent as flags floating on the wind.

Wagons creaked as the wood and metal contracted in the cool air.

In the sky, a meteor fell, streaking across the sky like a striking match.

John Masters threw sand on the fire, smothering its flame. The coals burned on, underneath.

He stood, for a moment, looking in the direction Gunn had gone.

Weary, he knew he could sleep. A man was out there.

A man he could trust.

A man called Gunn.

CHAPTER TEN

The wind rose over the hot dry land as if summoned. A cool wind, out of the north, a vestige of winter in that Texas spring. And still the night lurked there, with its clear sky and brittle sparkling stars, its shell-curve of a moon, its nighthawks and bats, its strand of Milky Way stretching across the heavens like a sash of silver dust.

Gunn lay there, on his blankets, staring up at the vast sky, unable to sleep. Not cold yet. Not cold enough to crawl under. His boots were off, handy. His gunbelt was rolled up, the butt of his pistol close to hand. The boots were under his blanket, raising it like a pillow. Spurs shoved in the ground so he wouldn't forget them in the morning. Belt loosened, hat nailed down by the brim with a pair of stones. Arms extended; hands locked behind his head.

Looking into the night, wondering. As he always wondered. Feeling small with all those stars scattered in the sky like lanterns. Mysterious. So many, and so far away. He could sense that. The distances. The oddness of them. Like the lights of a town. A big, sprawled-out town. A town no one would ever see. A city so huge it would take many lifetimes to ride through on a horse.

His eyelids dipped, as sleepiness nudged him. He became aware of his aching muscles, of the tension draining away like silt on his shoulders as he bathed in a mountain stream. A good feeling.

From afar, a rabbit screamed. A high-pitched

squeal. Owl. Coyote. Snake. Some creature had gotten the rabbit. Life. It made sense in a way if you took every piece and played it like cards. Or fitted it together like a jigsaw puzzle. He thought of the Sioux, whom he had come to know. To them, everything was alive: a stone, a river, a tree, a star. Yes, it made sense. It was difficult to understand, but if you took what they said as truth, everything he saw now made perfect sense. He could feel the ground beneath him. Alive. With doodle bugs, scorpions, tiny grains of sand that moved when he moved, smaller bugs that no one could see. Spiders, lizards, millions of heartbeats all pulsing like the stars, all plucked to a hidden rhythm by an unseen hand.

He dozed, his thoughts straying, streaming beyond him in his weariness as if they were tumbleweeds scurried along by the breeze that sighed over him like a furry creature with no shape, no form. Cool as a hand across his brow, gentle as a touch by a woman's delicate fingers.

His eyelids grew heavy as iron stove lids.

The sky came down on him, like a big blanket, like a friend, and he fell asleep on top of his bedroll, the cool breeze washing over him sweet as anything he had ever known. The last strand of thought was a fragment of a vision he had once had: an Indian girl speaking to him in sign about how everything in the world, in the sky, was all woven together like a brilliant blanket and there was no need to worry about anything . . . ever . . . ever, or at all . . .

Laura Masters lay in the covered wagon, her heart pounding.

Betsy had tossed and turned for what seemed like hours, but was finally asleep. Her mother was breathing very evenly, but she didn't know if she was asleep or not.

The cool breeze blew through the openings, but Laura could not feel the cool. She swarmed with desire. A hot, irrational desire. A crazy desire that stirred her loins, triggered unclean thoughts in her mind. Lustful thoughts. About a man she did not know, but who was like a powerful lodestone, drawing her to him. She put a hand to her breast as if to quieten the sound of her pounding heart. She was almost certain her mother could hear it thumping under her swollen breast. Could hear her controlled breathing. Could read her lustful thoughts.

"Mother?" she whispered.

No answer.

Laura's heart thrummed hard against the walls of her chest, pulsed in the concave hollow of her throat above the rib-cage.

She thought of Gunn, somewhere out there in the dark night, well away from the other sleepers.

"Ma?"

Again, no answer.

Carefully, slowly, Laura slid from under the covers. She wore a petticoat, but grabbed a dress from the bundle of clothing at her feet. She kept her eyes on the sleeping forms as she climbed out the back of the wagon. Quickly, she pulled the dress over her head, shook it straight. The camp was quiet. The other wagons, the men, were some distance away. Her father, she knew, would be sleeping near the supply wagon where the rifles and ammunition were packed.

She knew what was driving her, making her act so insane. The dream. A dream that had haunted her for years, ever since she had passed puberty. It was crazy, but the moment she had seen Gunn, she had known that she must surrender herself to him. The dream was more than just a passing image during sleep. She had dreamed such a man in the daytime, too. A tall man, ruggedly handsome, with soft pale eyes. She shuddered now, thinking of Gunn; his grey eyes.

Her bare feet were on the ground. She hung on to the gate of the wagon for a moment, trembling.

No one moved inside the wagon.

She reached back over the gate, found her moccasins. Quickly, she slipped them on. She looked around, saw no one, heard no sound, except the muffled snort of a horse, the *clack* of a hoof against stone.

Laura held her breath, moved away from the wagon. Her feet padded on the earth, making the faintest of sounds. Her heart made more noise than she did, she was sure. She kept the image of Gunn strong in her mind, for courage, and remembered the direction he had walked, alone, after supper. Once away from the camp, she moved faster, arrowing toward the north almost by instinct.

She thought of Gunn out there alone, that last image of him clear in her mind: walking away with his bedroll tucked under his arm, his long stride carrying him out of sight over the knoll. He was out there now, in the dark.

She thought of Betsy, who had lain with him, and the way his trousers hugged his thighs. She thought of the bulge at the crotch of his pants, pushing against the tight-fitting denim.

She hated herself, forgave herself in a single instant. Pangs of desire flooded her, stabbed her, smothered her. But what was wrong in that? In having that desire? Was not this the way it should be? Gunn was a man; she was a woman. It was tiresome and frustrating waiting always for the right man to come along. The years slipped by and she could end up a spinster if she did not find her man. Betsy was sowing her wild oats, at least, and did not cry herself to sleep at night. She envied Betsy in a way, and now she was about to emulate her. Be bold, go for a man she was drawn to, instead of hiding behind her mother's skirts, instead of sitting at home with that terrible longing in her heart.

She thought of her father, sleeping back there under the supply wagon. She had long ago ceased to question why her father and mother seemed so much in love yet seldom slept in the same bed together. Those mysterious night noises, the odd sounds, had stopped a long time ago. Their lives now were almost separate, were separate at night, and invisible barriers between them locked in their secrets.

Her boldness flagged as she wondered if Gunn might not even be where she thought he would. What if he was not there? After all, she didn't know where he was going to sleep. Somewhere north of the camp, near the wide rutted trail. Maybe he would shoot her, mistaking her for a prowler. Maybe he would send her away. The last thought was too miserable to keep in her mind. She didn't know if she could take his rejection.

Last Spring she had tried being nice to a man, but he was an odd one who looked right through her. Turned out that he had lived among Indians for so long that he was frightened of white women, didn't know how to act around them. The experience had done nothing for her confidence, especially after Betsy had found out about it and teased her mercilessly.

Laura picked her way through the dark, suddenly afraid of snakes. Several times she considered turning back, but the heat of her desire was still strong.

Her feelings now were the strangest she had ever had. There was something about Gunn that drew her to him. A hardess in him that hid a softness; the hint of a tender core underneath that flint look in his pale grey eyes.

She almost gasped aloud when she saw the dark shape near some rocks, a few yards east of the trail. She approached, heard the sound of his breathing. Regular, even, steady. She dared not speak, not yet. Her heart throbbed in the hollow of her throat. Her calves quivered as desire once again flooded her loins.

Carefully, she moved still closer to the sleeping man.

He lay on his back, unmoving, his eyes closed, the lids dusted with the silver light of stars. She crept closer on moccasined feet until she stood above him, trying desperately to control her breathing.

The breeze ebbed for a moment and she drew in a breath, gazed upon his serene countenance, shadowed by the night itself, faintly limned by star and moon-glow. The earth seemed to draw breath too, and this gave her courage.

His blankets were spread wide on the ground. There was room for her. Boldly, she sat down next to the sleeping man. He seemed so big, so powerful, even in repose. She could smell his masculine musk. Fear clutched at her throat, wallowed in her stomach like some slithering beast. Yet this served only to increase her desire. An image of him holding, kissing her, filled her mind.

She reached a hand toward him. Her fingertips lightly touched the bulge at his crotch. She slid her palm over the mass. She could feel the heat in her hand. Gently, she rubbed the mount of hidden flesh, caressing it as her loins quivered with desire. Laura felt an electric tingle shoot up her arm as she stroked Gunn's protruding genitals. The soft mound began to harden. Excitement tingled her veins. Her heart raced. Clenching her teeth, she told herself that it would be "now or never." Marveling at her own boldness, she unfastened the top button of his trousers, then the one beneath it. The third button popped from its hole without any help from her. Her fingers touched the swollen cock as it snapped out of its coiled lethargy, stiffened like an arrow pointing at Gunn's belly button. The mushroomed head of it poked free of his shorts. She touched the crown of it almost reverently, felt its velvety smoothness. A dampness seeped through her panties, soaked through her pubic hairs, oiled her inner thighs. Her legs and hips felt drained of strength, almost numb. She grew weak with an overpowering excitement.

Laura slipped her hand inside Gunn's shorts, felt the swollen length of his cock, bumpy with engorged veins. Felt the veined bulk of it, grew rapturous over its size, imagined its potency. She longed to grasp it, squeeze it, caress it. She stretched out beside him, enervated with desire, listened to his even breathing, hoping he would not wake up just yet.

She lay next to him, her fingers resting gently on his manhood. She touched the tip of the crown again, felt the warm seep of fluid. She tasted it on the tip of her tongue. The taste was lemony, tart. Fascinated, she leaned close, stuck out her tongue. She dabbled the head of his cock with her tongue. A warm thrill immediately flooded through her. Emboldened, she lifted the organ, pulled the crown into the steaming cave of her mouth.

Gunn jolted awake, startling her.

"Huh?" he groaned. "What the . . ."

"Shh!" she whispered. "I mean no harm. I—I just had to come here, touch you."

Gunn shook off sleep, widened his eyes. He was groggy, disoriented. He saw the dark silhouette of a woman's head framed against the sky, felt the hard ground under his back.

"Betsy?"

Laura laughed nervously.

"No. It's me. Her sister."

"Laura?"

"Yes."

Gunn sat up, reached out, touched her face. He put a hand on his lap, confirmed his suspicions that his fly was open, his penis crawling out of his shorts.

"Good lord, woman, do you want to get me shot?"

"Please! No one knows I'm here. I had to come. I know you like Betsy and were with her, but I don't care. I want you too. Is what I'm doing so wrong?"

"Some people might think so," Gunn said drily. "Including your father and your mother. You're taking a hell of a chance coming here like this, Laura."

She drew in a quick breath. She was still excited; more excited than before now that the cat was out of the bag.

"I know, but we can do it. I—I won't stay long. Just a little while. Please?"

She slid up to him, touched his face with her hand. Her fingers roamed the flat planes of his face, made a scratching sound on his chin.

Gunn let out a weary sigh. This was unexpected, but not exactly something that had never happened to him before. That it was Laura, and not Betsy, surprised him, but he could live with that. He drew in her scent, felt his manhood respond as fresh blood flooded the veins. He grabbed her roughly, drew her to him. He kissed her on the lips, shivered as his loins spasmed with a twinge. She responded, melting into him, her breasts mashing against his chest like tiny cushions.

–He knew the risks. If John Masters found them like this he wouldn't ask any questions. He'd horsewhip them both on the spot—or worse, shoot him. He might be so deranged he would shoot them both. It was a tricky situation. But Laura was soft and willing. Her breath was hot in his mouth. Her hair tickled his face. Her body began to move as he kissed her. She was supple in his arms, passionate, full of a yearning that transmitted electricity to her touch.

"Get out of your dress," he husked.

"Yes, oh yes," she breathed.

Gunn slid out of his trousers and shorts.

That was naked enough to do what he was going to do. He watched her raise her arms, pulled the dress over her head. She slithered out of her petticoat. Her breasts tumbled free. He helped her tug off her panties, felt the dampness in the thick nest between her legs. He touched her pubes, stroked them with gentle, probing fingers. She quivered every time he touched her. He lay her on her back, slid her under his blanket.

Her hands explored his flesh, plucking at him as if kneading dough. He kissed her breasts, tongued the nipples hard. His hand continued to squeeze her genital lips, his finger plied the wet sucking mouth of her portal, slid to the clitoris. He stroked it until she bucked with pleasure, gasping, her fingers pulling at his flesh in loving desperation.

"Oh, Gunn, I'm so hot. Do it to me quick. I can't wait any longer."

He climbed onto her body, found the target with his cock. It slid past the swollen lips of her sex, into the oiled tunnel. It was all velvet and heat, a delicious wetness that drenched his organ, squeezed it with undulating muscles. She drew him in deep and he realized that she was no virgin.

106

"Ah," he said.

"Oh, yes. That's what I want. What I've always wanted. I dreamed of you, Gunn. Dreamed of you loving me like this."

"Me?"

"You. Someone just like you. I—I gave myself to others, hoping it was you, but it wasn't. This is real. This is the way I dreamed it."

He plumbed her deep, stroked back and forth over the hardened tip of her tingle. With each stroke, she bucked and creamed. Her body was quick and lively under the covers.

Her fingers kneaded his back as if she was trying to climb inside it, make their bodies one.

She urged him to go faster and faster until he was driving into her with all the force he could muster. Her honey flowed until he was swimming inside her. But her muscles clasped him, squeezed his rock-hard cock until he felt his seed rally to burst from its emprisoning sac. He tried desperately to stay the final moment, but she triggered his orgasm with a single, surprising phrase.

"Fuck me, Gunn, fuck me forever!"

His loins smacked into hers as he plunged deep with a single furious stroke.

A cloud-stream of seed shot up from his scrotum, burst from him like a hot surge of milk.

She cried out, screamed softly in his ear.

Her fingers stopped moving, dug in, quivered.

Laura spasmed. Again and again as he shuddered the last of his milky seed into her womb.

"Yes, Gunn," she whispered. "Thank you. It was you. All the time it was you."

"Huh?" he gasped, spent, lying on her in exhaustion.

"You were the man I always dreamed of. You are

my dream, come to life."

CHAPTER ELEVEN

Gee-Haw Winesap was the next man to drop when the phantom rifle boomed.

The Masters expedition had just crossed the Brazos without incident when it happened. Gee-Haw was walking away from the noon meal to relieve himself. He went over a hill into an arroyo.

Someone was waiting for him. The big buffalo gun shattered the silence. The bullet caught Gee-Haw in the throat, same as the one that had killed Earl Pettibone. Gee-Haw crawled twenty feet before his blood ran out.

Everyone from the camp came running. No one saw anything. Gordie Winesap picked up his brother, tried to close the throat wound with his hands, but he knew it was no use. Gee-Haw was gone, his body limp in his brother's arms.

Gunn ran down to the end of the arroyo in the direction Gee-Haw was crawling when he died. He snatched up the forked stick stuck into the ground, examined the tracks. This time he had footprints to read. Boots sunk deep in the soft sandy earth, fresh enough to tell him a little. A big man, fairly new boots, wide heels, rounded toes. He knew he was wasting valuable time, but he had to know if only one man was involved and if it was the same man.

The horse's tracks told him that the same man who had killed Pettibone had also murdered Winesap. And, he had kept the horse near while he had set up for the kill. As soon as he had fired, he had mounted up, ridden away. The shooter had not waited to see if his shot was true. It was, and the bastard had known it would be when he fired.

He liked to go for the throat.

And he didn't miss.

"Jed!" Gunn called. "Bring my horse quick!"

From where he stood, Gunn could see the crowd trying to console Gordie in his grief. Masters broke away from the bunch, started walking toward him. When he came up, Gunn handed him the forked stick.

"He used this."

Masters looked at it, turned it over in his hands. He gave close scrutiny to the way the branch was cut, the long center piece whittled to a point.

"Willow," he said. "Likely cut back there on the banks of the Brazos."

"Anything different about it?"

"Anyone of a dozen men could have cut this branch. Think you can catch the man?"

"No, but I have to try. Maybe his horse will step into a prairie dog hole, break a leg. I'll give it an hour or so, let you know what I find out."

"Good. Gordie's taking this pretty hard. It ain't settlin' well with the others neither. Damned bushwacker's got my outfit half spooked."

"You think it might be one of the Simons bunch?"

"Who else?"

Jed rode up on his own horse, leading Esquire.

"Want me to ride with you, Gunn?"

"No, this is my party."

Gunn mounted his horse, saluted Masters, rode off through the mouth of the arroyo, climbed to high ground. Again, he lost the tracks in the maze on the main trail. It was discouraging, but expected. He did not turn back, but waited for the Masters party to catch up. When Masters was close enough to see him, Gunn shook his head and continued to ride point. His eyes swept the broken landscape looking for a telltale cloud of dust, but whoever had shot Gee-Haw had gotten clean away.

Two hours later, he found a dry camp by the side of the trail. He had almost missed it. There were three sets of horse tracks at the camp. Men had spent the night there. They had smoked cigarettes, chewed tobacco, spread out their bedrolls. Two of the men had ridden north long before the other man had headed south, back to the place of ambush. Those tracks matched the ones he had seen at the Colorado and the Brazos crossings.

It was puzzling.

If these men were with the Simons bunch, they were lagging well behind. The way the loose sand filled the tracks told him how long ago they had been at the camp. The bushwacker had not returned here. There was no reason for him to; he had ridden on ahead, probably to rejoin his two companions.

But who were they? And why was one of them, probably the best marksman of the three, cutting down Masters' men one by one? Were they trying to demoralize the men who rode for Masters? Were they hired killers sent to discourage Masters from continuing on his expedition? A lone man, nursing a grudge?

The man was smart. He knew the best places to wait. He had to have watched the Masters caravan stop for lunch, picked that arroyo as a likely place for someone to use for a nature call. If so, that still didn't explain why Gee-Haw was shot. It was as if the ambusher would have shot anybody who walked into that arroyo. It could have just as well have been

Masters himself. Or one of the women. Gunn shuddered to think that Laura or Betsy or Evie would have been shot had they gone to that particular arroyo.

Kurt Simons shook like a dog shitting peach seeds.

The last kill had been the chanciest he had ever taken. The sweetest shot he had ever made, but the most dangerous, too. Setting up the forked stake as a rifle rest, waiting. The target coming into the sights of the big buffalo gun. The Freund Sharps in fifty caliber. He could drop a buffalo at 800 yards or more with the single-shot weapon. At three hundred yards, the almost one-ounce lead ball could drop the toughest bull.

Wayne and Lefty would have been mighty proud. Seeing him hold his breath, squeeze the trigger. Gee-Haw falling as if pole-axed, kicking in the dirt. A perfect throat shot. A man couldn't yell and he couldn't live long after such a shot.

He couldn't wait to tell them. But the ride out of the arroyo had been hairy. The boom of the rifle still echoed in his eardrums. The galloping hooves making a sound louder than thunder. Even now, he looked back over his shoulder to see if the whole camp was on his ass.

There was a deep thrill, killing this way. A bigger kick than any buffalo run. This was big game. Human game. The hardest bag of all.

He swung off the trail, headed for Fort Worth. He could breathe easier now. There had been no dust behind him for the last hour. Once he caught up with his brothers, he'd be safe. No one could prove anything. They'd swear he had been with them all the time. Nobody could say different. But it was that damned Gunn he wanted. The bastard was a tracker.

If it worked out, he'd track himself right into a perfect ambush. Let him come on. He was ready.

Wayne and Lefty rode up to meet him, just outside Fort Worth, as they had planned.

Kurt waved, grinned.

"Did you get one?" asked Wayne.

"Damned if I didn't. Gee-Haw!"

"Gee-Haw Winesap!" exclaimed Lefty. "That ought to slow 'em some."

"Gunn lit out after me, but he never caught up." Kurt looked over his shoulder just the same, as if to reassure himself.

"I'll ride on ahead, tell Pa," said Wayne. "Y'all comin'?"

"I want one more before we get to the Cimarron," said Kurt. "Oh, you ought to have seen that shot! Gee-haw never knew what hit him!" Kurt told them the whole story as they rode along. Afterwards, Wayne spurred his horse, rode on to catch up to the wagons. Kurt and Lefty stopped long enough to swig some canteen water, build smokes. In Fort Worth, Kurt bought a pint to pack with him. He and Lefty celebrated with a couple of drinks for good measure.

"One more night out in the open and we ought to be finished with Masters," boasted Kurt.

"You figger he'll turn back?"

Kurt chewed on that for a while. Masters was not the type of man to spook easy. But by the time he had lost three good men he ought to get the idea that he was not welcome up on the Cimarron. Few men would want to buck such odds. It could be, though, that Masters would take it real personal and jump to conclusions. He might want a hide for a hide.

"He'll be mighty sorry if he don't," said Kurt. "Come on. I want to set up my next stand on the Red. Masters will be so damned leery of rivers he'll think twice before he crosses the Cimarron after buff."

Lefty laughed, but it was a forced, hard laugh, the kind a man makes after he hears a sound in an empty room during the night. You know there's no one there, but something was there and you laugh at yourself for being scared of nothing.

Jed Randall caught up with Gunn. His horse's hide was sleek with sweat, blowing hard through rubbery nostrils. Randall called out, breathlessly.

"Hold up, man!"

Gunn had been so absorbed in tracking that Jed startled him. He reined in, sat on Esquire as Randall loped up.

"Masters wants you back. Sent me up here. Hell, Gunn, I must've rode ten mile to catch you. They buried that Winesap and John's been spittin' nails ever since. I bet if you touched him you'd burn your hand."

"I might catch up to the killer in Fort Worth. I could be there in another hour or so."

"That's the point," Jed panted. "Masters don't want to go to Fort Worth. He's got riders out ever'where. He practically promised everyone that there'd be no more killings. He claims to swing wide, check the banks of ever' river we cross from here to the Cimarron."

"Might not be a bad idea," Gun agreed.

"He swung way off, wants us to meet him this side of the Red."

"I don't think he'll have any more trouble this soon after Gee-Haw. But whoever's doing the shooting is damned sure staying close to the rivers."

"I wonder why he didn't shoot Gee-Haw on the Brazos, then, but waited until after we crossed it."

"Could be that he's getting big for his britches. He's

113

either crazy or a show-off."

Gunn fished the makings from his pocket. He slid a paper loose, poured tobacco in the trough he made with his fingers. He handed the sack of tobacco to Jed, rolled the tobacco tight, licked the paper edge. He folded the other edge onto the wet edge, stroked it up and down its length to seal the tobacco inside. He struck a match, lit their cigarettes. Gunn inhaled the smoke deeply as his eyes swept the horizon. To the east he saw the faint haze left by dust from the Masters wagons. It was a good fifteen miles to the river bank where they would intercept Masters. They'd be there well before dark if they rode steady. No need to hurry. Masters might want to cross the Canadian before dark or wait until morning.

One thing was sure. Someone would have to sweep the opposite bank and beyond before the main body of the expedition traveled the trail. Someone would have to be out there ahead of the bunch making sure no one was waiting in ambush. Every stop from now on would have to be picked carefully and guards posted at each location.

"I woke up early this morning," said Randall. "Saw a mighty peculiar thing. At first I thought it was a haunt, but when I saw her climb into the covered wagon, I realized it was just a woman with only a petticoat on."

"Sure you weren't dreaming, Jed?"

"No, because she got caught on the wagon, her petticoat did, and I had to get out of my soogan and help her get loose. It was Laura Masters and she was in a heap of trouble."

"Anybody else see her? Her mother or sister wake up?"

Jed grinned.

Gunn wanted to knock him out of the saddle.

114

Randall was enjoying his little story too damned much.

"Nope. You got lucky, Gunn. But I wouldn't make a habit of it. Laura spoke to me before I rode out here and said her ma was mighty suspicious. Seems Laura's hair was full of twigs and sand and all that this morning. She said to tell you that everything was O.K. She told her ma she was sleepwalking."

"Yair," said Gunn. "Maybe she was."

He kicked spurs into Esquire's flanks, rode slightly ahead of Randall. Jed would understand that sometimes a man had to be alone, even in company. Mention of Laura had triggered memories, dredged up hopes and dreams he had tried to bury after his wife Laurie's death. He was still surprised that a woman like Laura would come to him, at some risk, and bed him without any urging on his part. And give herself so willingly. So lovingly.

Gunn had no illusions about Laura Masters. He did not know her at all. Yet he felt something for her. Maybe it was only a fragment of feeling left over from the old dream. Maybe it was only the wishful thinking of a drifter, who had no ties and still thought of Arkansas and Osage Creek, Fairview township, where the grass grew high and the chiggers red as chili peppers, twice as hot on the ankles, the ticks thick and fat as turnips, the copperheads sleek as an oiled rifle barrel, fish in the streams, hills bright as emeralds in summer, solemn and bare as an empty church in winter, threaded by cautious deer stepping through the skeletons of leaves, their nostrils blowing smoke, their ears stiff-perked as corn husks shucked on the stalks.

He could feel her soft body now, spongy as a cotton pile. He recalled her breasts, the wonder of them in the dark, the mystery of her nipples as they hardened between his lips. He thought of the way her hips moved, the way their bodies fit together like stacked spoons in a drawer.

The fountains inside her. The warm grasp of her sex when he was buried deep inside her love-tunnel. The rasp of her nest of hairs against his manhood as it slid through the wiry thatch to the wet warmth of her womb. The mouthy depths suckling him even deeper, the tender pain at the crown of his cock when he shot his milky seed.

She had not lingered, as he had half-hoped. True to her promise, she had risen from the blankets, pulled on her petticoat, gathered her clothes and padded back to her wagon. Leaving him with a bittersweet ache that burned at his heart like a sulphur match. He had wanted to rise up, too, and follow her, bring her back, give up his wandering life for the home he remembered, wanted, sometimes, so bad he had to fight back the tears.

But something inside him had hardened, steeled him to silence.

Laura could have been anyone. Anyone at all.

Was she the someone he might want to share his blankets, build a home for, start all over again for?

He tried now to see her face in his mind.

Indistinct impressions. Betsy, Evie—Laura. Something in his head blocking any sure vision of Laura. She was like faint spoor of a doe near a creek. When the water ran hard, the tracks faded, swirled away forever.

Gun stopped up short. This was madness. The sun boiling his brain.

Jed rode up, curious.

"You all right, Gunn?"

Gunn looked at his friend, his grey eyes narrowed to dark wedges.

"You hear anything?" he said.

Jed shook his head.

Gunn's eyes swept the path ahead. Trees dotted the rolling land, patternless, the growth broken up by the gullies, rain-creeks, flood scars.

Sometimes a man can be thinking and a shadow will pass over the sun. A cloud, or nothing at all.

Gunn felt this way now.

He had seen nothing. Heard nothing.

Yet, small hairs prickled on his neck.

"You hold up, Jed, snake out your rifle."

"What for? There ain't a doubledamned thing out there."

Jed looked all around, his eyes bulging like white-washed plums. He stood up in the stirrups, scanned the circumference of earth and sky.

Gunn slid the Winchester out of its scabbard, hammered it back. There was a shell in the chamber, had been ever since the Gee-Haw had bought a dirty hole and some stones to mark his grave.

The smack of sound crackled the air.

Bright orange flame blossomed two hundred yards away. A puff of smoke rose in the air like a ghost.

Jed jerked in the saddle. A whiz-sound sizzled behind the hard *thunk* of lead cracking into flesh.

Gunn raised his rifle, then ducked as another rifle-snap warned him that a bullet was on the way. Out of the corner of his eye, he saw the brief orange flare and then the white smoke blot out the shooter.

A lead ball burned past his ear with a deadly hiss, like an iron horseshoe, heated to cherry red, dipping into the blacksmith's water barrel.

And then the rider rose up out of a gully, and charged toward him as he saw Jed Randall teeter out of the saddle, his arm running with bright blood.

117

CHAPTER TWELVE

Gordie Winesap had come to kill a man.

A man called Gunn.

Slobber drooled down his chin as he jacked another shell into the chamber of the Winchester. Had he missed? Smoke and sweat blotted out his vision. He ran the back of his hand over his brows, tried to see if Gunn had fallen from his saddle.

He had it all figured out, although no one would listen to him. He had tried to talk it all out with Curly Cow Charlie, but Charlie hadn't listened. Gunn was a damned Jonah. He had to be the reason the Simons were picking them off one by one. That trouble back in San Antonio with Wayne Simons. And then, as he had heard, with Kurt. The Simons had to be behind the shootings. Gee-Haw dead because of a damned stranger!

Gordie looked down the barrel of his rifle again, tried to bring the tall man into his sights. The big sorrel galloped off at an angle and it appeared that no one was in the saddle. Jed Randall was turning his horse back. Well, he had no quarrel with Randall, even though he was a friend of Gunn's. He wasn't the same kind of man. Gunn was a hardcase and a troublemaker. A jinx.

Gee-Haw hadn't asked to be killed. Neither had Pettibone. Two good men gone and no good reason.

He had tried to tell Charlie that. It was plain that Masters thought Gunn was trouble, too. Else why did he always send Gunn out to ride point or sleep outside

of camp? Hell, it was plain. John Masters knew
something was wrong. Gunn had said something to
one of the Simons boys and now they wanted revenge.
They hadn't meant to kill Gee-Haw. They was after
the stranger with the pale eyes like pewter buttons
sewed to a doll's face. Jesus, he had never seen eyes
like that. Cold as an October frost, wild as an
untamed mustang's when the rope first snakes around
his neck. A man like that was no damned good. He
brought trouble with him sure as a black cloud brings
rain or hail. John Masters had no business hiring such
a man. Once he was dead, there'd be no more trouble
on this run. No more killings.

Gordie's eyes closed for a moment as he fought back
tears. He could no longer see where Gunn's big horse
had gone. He rubbed his dust-caked face, dabbed at
the line of sweat rimming the bags under his eyes. His
thumb idly stroked the hammer of the Winchester.

It had not been easy getting away from Masters and
the others, but he had managed. Something had
snapped in his mind when he had heard John give the
orders to change their route. He had called young
Randall up, told him to find and fetch Gunn, have
the stranger meet them on the south bank of the
Canadian River. Curly Cow Charlie had been riding
in the wagon with him, taking Gee-Haw's place. He
had said he was choking on the dust, handed the reins
to Charlie and gotten a horse to ride. Followed
Randall, then doubled back here to wait for Gunn to
show.

There was no sign of Gunn nor his horse. It was as if
the earth had swallowed them up.

Gunn hung on to his horse, hugging its belly.

The sound of the last bullet whizzing by still rang in
his ears. He worked the reins, bringing Esquire

between him and the bushwacker.

"Jed, listen careful," he said. "I'm going to try and flank that bastard. Want you to hold up until I give the signal. But move back out of range."

"What you aim to do?"

"Sneak up on him, if I can."

"Why don't you just kill the sonofabitch?"

"Because I want some information from him. I want to know who he is and why he's out here shooting at us."

"You figure he's the same one what shot Pettibone and Winesap?"

"Maybe. But he's not using a buffalo gun. That's a Winchester, most likely."

"A thirty caliber can kill just the same as a fifty."

"Move on back. I'm going to drift north, circle behind him. When you see my signal, you ride straight for where you last saw the smoke. Keep him busy."

"What if he shoots me?"

"I'll be real sorry, Jed."

Gunn clucked to his horse, prodded his flank with a spur. His arm ached where he hung on to the saddle horn. One leg gripped the opposite flank, the knee touching the cantle. Esquire stepped out, followed the path dictated by the tug of the bit in his mouth. Randall rode out to a spot some four hundred yards distant from where the puff of smoke turned to wisps.

It took Gunn a good twenty minutes to disappear completely.

He moved down a gulley, then angled west. When he had gone far enough, he turned Esquire back south. If he had figured correctly, he would be slightly west of the bushwacker's position. He hunched low in the saddle, waited until he saw the tops of the trees. He smiled. He had made a circle, undetected. If the

120

ambusher was still in the same position, Gunn had both flanked him and come up behind him.

He slid to the ground, pulled the Winchester from its scabbard. He wrapped the reins around a mesquite bush, crept toward the trees on foot, staying low. He had to cross a small gully. He started down it, slipped. Fell. A stone rattled, broken loose by his fall.

Gunn froze.

He moved on up the other side of the ditch, peered over it. He saw the man in the trees looking around, sunlight sparkling off the barrel of his rifle. He could not see his face. Gunn waited until the man relaxed, shifted his gaze toward Jed Randall.

It seemed to take hours to climb out of the gully, stalk the ambusher. He moved a step at a time, picking his way carefully. At one point, he crouched behind a knoll, listening. A careful man would seldom be seen if he changed his usual shape, moved very little. If he moved not at all such a man would be almost impossible to see except by an experienced hunter. Even then, the hunter would have to be searching for a man and not some other animal. Gunn knew that the man he stalked was probably a hunter. He hunched his back, moved a cautious step at a time. Waited, stepped. Waited.

He was close now.

Beyond, in the distance, he could see Jed Randall patiently sitting his horse. The earth danced with shimmering heat waves. Randall was a blurred man on an indistinct animal, little more than an illusion. The bushwacker was clearly visible from behind, his head moving slowly from side to side as if scanning the land for movement. The man was a hunter, or used to seeking game in difficult places. He did not move much, and his horse sat still for him as if divining the man's intent. For a moment, Gunn was tempted to shoot him out of the saddle and ride on, leaving the man's bones to bleach in the sun. But he had never back-shot a man in his life and he would not change his pattern now. But the hatred in him boiled to the surface now that he thought of what might have happened had the man been more accurate. He, Gunn, could be dead now. Randall, too.

Gunn readied his rifle.

Not to shoot, but to signal with to Jed. And, after that, to use to bring the man in the trees down, but alive.

He stood at the top of a rise, brought his rifle up so that its barrel would catch the sun. He moved it in an arc, a half-circle. The barrel glistened as sunlight bounced off its metal surface. He sank into a crouch again, the rifle held hip-high ready to cock and shoot if the bushwacker detected his presence and turned.

The man in the trees did not move.

Randall charged.

From four hundred yards away, Jed whipped his horse into a gallop, whooped loudly.

Gunn moved fast toward the man in the trees.

Twenty yards away, Gunn slowed, ready for any aggressive movement from the man who had shot at him.

Gordie Winesap continued to stare at Randall. He raised his rifle to his shoulder, thumbed the hammer back. He took aim. To Gunn's surprise, the man raised the barrel, fired. He shot over Randall's head!

Dumbstruck, Gunn stared hard at the man's back. Then, he lowered his head and started running toward the bushwacker.

Gordie half-turned in the saddle. He saw Gunn coming towards him. He started to swing his rifle, cock it at the same time. In that instant, Gunn recognized his attacker. He bounded six feet in a single jump, shifted the rifle in his hands until both hands clasped the barrel.

Winesap shouted something.

Gunn reached the stirrup, swung hard with the rifle. The butt stock slammed into Gordie's elbow, knocking the rifle from his hands. It flipped to the ground, hit with a rattling of metal and stone. Gordie screamed in pain, reeled backwards.

Gunn reached up with one hand, grabbed his shirt. He jerked him forward, pulled him out of the saddle. As Gordie fell, Gunn released him. Winesap hit the ground with a sickening thud.

Jed Randall rode up, his face drained of blood.

"Jesus," he said, "that's Gordie Winesap. I thought he was on our side."

Gordie groaned in pain.

Gunn stepped up to him, leaned down. He cocked his rifle, shoved the barrel in the man's face. Gunn's jaw hardened to stone.

"You've got about one minute to explain, feller," he said quietly, "or I blow you straight to hell."

CHAPTER THIRTEEN

John Masters followed the course of the Brazos west, then turned the wagons north. They reached the Red River well before dusk, but the weariness was beginning to show in the men. The women seemed to have renewed energy by the time they had set up camp, started the cooking fires. There was no sign of Gunn or Randall. No one had said much about Gordie Winesap, but he was on everybody's mind.

"Well, boys we're on the border," said Masters. "From here on, we scout for buff."

Curly Cow Charlie stood above the bank, a Sharps cradled in his arms. He scanned the opposite bank, grunted his approval. Masters had brought them to a place where there was not much concealment on the other shore. They could ford here if it didn't flood during the night. Still, he was worried.

"Reckon we ought to cross tonight?" he asked Masters.

"We'll wait for Gunn and Randall."

"What about Gordie?" asked a skinner named Sid Blanton. "You talked to him, Charlie. What'd he say again?'

"It ain't important." Masters shot him a look. The men were all sitting in a circle, their immediate chores out of the way. The Mexican wrangler had the horses and mules all hobbled, was squatted in view of them, a cigarette dangling from his lips. He, like the others, looked as if he'd waded through a buffalo wallow. They were all waiting to get to the river after dark and swim naked out of sight of the womenfolks.

"I think it is important," insisted Sid. "This Gunn may be a Jonah like Gordie said."

The men muttered their approval. Most of them. The Mexican squinted into the falling sun and drew deeply on his cigarette. A horse snorted, started toward the river. The Mexican lifted his arm, waved the animal back.

"Look," said Masters, sensing trouble, "Gordie has something in his craw, I'll grant you that. But he's way off his tether about this. Gunn is just an ordinary man trying to help out. Let's not look for trouble. We got enough as it is."

Sid stood up. His joints creaked. He was a lean, small man, with corded muscles. He was wiry, dark, in his early forties. He had a perpetually pinched face, beady dark eyes. He looked at the Mexican sharply.

"You gave Gordie a horse, Pedro. He say anything to you?"

The Mexican looked startled. Suddenly he was the center of attention.

He shrugged.

"Come on, Pablo, you know something," said Sid, pushing. The other men turned on the Mexican, fixed him with accusing eyes.

"He said he gonna kill this Gunn because he bad luck. But he won't kill this man, I think."

"Huh? What you gettin' at, Mex?" asked another man who was called Blackie.

"He has the sombra, the shadow. You cannot kill such a man easy, I think."

"Bullshit," said Sid.

"Maybe not," said Charlie. "This child has heard of such men. South of the border. They say if a man has the shadow following him he is dangerous and hard to kill. Like somethin's pertectin' him."

Masters looked at the men. They were suddenly very quiet. Charlie's words carried some weight. The problem wasn't resolved, but the talk had sobered them up some. It was time to nip the bud.

"That's enough of this talk," said Masters "Blackie, you get a rifle, scout that river good up and down. Sid, you keep an eye peeled to the south for anyone riding up."

There was some grumbling, but Masters had weeded out two of the men who were likely to cause trouble with their tongues.

"Pablo," said Masters, "when you finish your smoke, break out some grain for the stock. Charlie, you come with me."

An hour later, Gunn, Randall and Gordie Winesap

rode up from the southeast, drawn there by the cook fires and the smell of grub on the twilight air. Sid Blanton came running up with the news.

"Here comes Gordie back. Them other two jaspers with him."

Evie and her daughters joined the ragged line of men who gathered for the arrival of the three men. John Masters strode up from the river where he had been washing up for supper. He watched, with the others, as Gordie, flanked by Gunn and Randall, rode in, his head bowed, his body sagging in the saddle.

They all noticed that Gordie was unarmed.

"What happened?" asked Masters.

"We had some trouble," said Gunn.

"Trouble? Hell, Gordie here tried to bushwack us."

Everyone began speaking at once. Masters shouted for silence. Gunn slid out of the saddle carrying Gordie's rifle. He tossed it to Curly Cow Charlie, who caught it deftly.

"Hold this for Gordie until he gets his senses back," said Gunn.

"Did you try and shoot Gunn?" asked Masters, staring at Winesap.

Gordie nodded.

No one said anything for a long time.

Randall dismounted, stared at Gunn for several seconds.

"Hell, ain't you gonna say nothin', Gunn? Why Gordie acted plumb loco. Gunn could have shot him dead, but he snuck up on him and knocked him silly. He would have killed Gunn though. He was throwin' down on him when Gunn jerked him out of his saddle."

"Let it go," said Gunn. "Gordie's had enough."

Masters looked at his wife. She understood. She walked up to Gordie's horse, looked up at him.

"Come on, Gordie," she said, "I'll get you a hot cup of coffee."

He stared at her, tears filling his eyes. He nodded dumbly. She stretched out her hand. He took it, threw a leg over the saddle and slid down. She walked away with him toward the chuck wagon as everyone stood around awkwardly.

"Sid," said Masters, "take care of Gordie's horse."

"Hold on now," said Blanton, "you just gonna let it go at that? Hell, this Gunn jasper's got a lot of explainin' to do, you ask me. Gordie's one of us. Gunn's the outsider."

Gunn said nothing, but his grey eyes flickered with warning.

"You better hold your tongue," said Randall, coming to Gunn's defense.

Masters stepped between the two men. He looked at Gunn, then at Blanton.

"I reckon we've had enough trouble for one day. There'll be no settlin' up anything now. You boys put up your horses and wash up for supper. We can talk later if anybody's still got anything in his craw."

Blanton angrily grabbed the reins of Gordie's horse. He glared at Gunn.

"This isn't finished yet," he grumbled.

The men and the two girls dispersed. Randall strode angrily toward the hobbled remuda, leading his horse.

Betsy and Laura stopped, looked back at Gunn. Laura smiled. Betsy waved, tentatively.

Gunn nodded to them, started toward the river to water his horse. His grey eyes smouldered like smoke trapped in a glass jar.

Kurt Simons beat Masters to the Red by the skin of his teeth. The Masters expedition was pushing to get thirty miles a day. Kurt had ridden fifty miles a day after leaving Fort Worth. His father and brothers crossed the Red a half day in front of him. They were already in Oklahoma, heading for the Canadian River where scouts had reported buffalo.

Kurt wasted another half day trying to find Masters.

When he saw the dust cloud, ten miles to the west, he grinned with satisfaction. He tucked the spy glass back in his saddle bags, rode wide of the north bank of the Red, raising no dust. By now, he reasoned, Masters would be wary. He'd have scouts out, pickets. As he rode into the sunset, he figured out his plan. The first ambush had worked because the wagons were in the river, helpless. He could pick his shot, with plenty of time to escape. When he shot the second man, surprise had been in his favor.

Now, however, he could not count on waiting for Masters to cross the river. Likely, he'd have scouts on the north bank long before he made the ford. Nor could he attack from the rear. They'd hunt him down quick.

But the river was still his best ally.

He marked the place where Masters set up camp. After the sun set, he could see the glow of the campfires. He made a dry camp near enough to hear voices drift across the river. Masters had made a mistake camping on that side of the Red. Had he crossed before dark, Kurt would have had to ride on to the Canadian and set up his ambush there. Now, he formulated the rest of his plans with confidence.

He sat there, in the trees as the stars winked out one by one. He watched for the glow of the fires to die down, the voices fade away.

An hour went by, while he listened to the nightsounds. The crunch of a boot on stone, the whisper of an owl as it glided past, hunting, the far-off yap of a coyote, a splash in the river. As the quiet deepened, Kurt knew it was time to reconnoiter. He would have to do it tonight, and he would have to do it right.

Kurt slipped a feed bag on his horse to keep him quiet, crawled to the river bank. Light shimmered on the waters of the Red. The air was clear and he could see the camp, ghostly in the moonlight. He heard the scrape of boots as men walked the picket line. Two men covered a quarter mile stretch, meeting at the camp, walking back separately in opposite directions.

That accounted for two men.

Were there more on guard?

He saw a match flare to the west, beyond the stopping point of the guard who walked in that direction. Kurt's scalp prickled. Another man there. Why? He wondered how many others were scattered away from camp. That could mean trouble for him.

He could wait here no longer. He had to make his guess at the distance across the river. This was not easy in the dark. Still, his rifle could reach, he was sure. He would have only one shot when the time came. He had to make it count, be ready to ride before they could muster arms against him. When the moment came to shoot, he would be exposed, vulnerable. That was the only kink in the rope.

Or was it? Now that he was here, so close, other problems presented themselves. Should he shoot from horseback?

What if Masters sent a man across the river before dawn?

Kurt Simons considered that possibility.

He'd have to take that man out, hoping there was only one. It would mean setting up in a different place. Farther north. It might work. He ran a tongue over dry lips. Might wasn't good enough. He'd have to be here all night. He would not be able to sleep. Even a nap could prove fatal.

Kurt began to feel his nerves fraying, shredding up like flakes from a wood plane. There was something spooky about lying so close to the Masters camp, planning to kill a man. No one to back him up. No one to discuss the plan with now nor in the morning.

The morning.

That's when he planned to bushwack the next man. Just at dawn, or before, when the camp started stirring. Before anyone had a chance to saddle a horse or look across the river. He would be exposed. Once he shot, the smoke and flame would give him away. He'd have to run for it, either on foot or on horseback. He had not made that decision yet. He would, after he'd mulled it through. A shot from horseback would be less sure. He needed to lie flat, take his time with aiming. But precious seconds would be lost if he had to run back to his horse, swing into the saddle and shove the rifle in its scabbard. Any man quick enough to find him in his sights could drop him while his back was turned, while he was running away.

He crawled along the bank, trying to find a place of concealment. A place that would also give him good support when he leveled the big Sharps. He found a clump of grass growing higher than the rest. A bush nearby. He rested on the tiny hillock, held his arms up as if there was a rifle in his hands. This place would work. It gave him a clean field of fire, some protection.

He saw the eastbound picket stop, look across at him. Kurt froze. He knew the man could not see him, but the feeling was eerie. He held his breath, waiting for the man to move on. When he did, Kurt let out his breath.

This place would have to do.

He scooted away from the bank, crawled west. Someone had struck a match on the other side. Past the quarter mile mark. He reached the point parallel to the place where he'd seen the match flare and peered into the darkness.

"Gunn?" someone called. The westbound picket.

"Yeah."

"You still awake?"

Kurt saw the glow of a cigarette then. Faint, tiny.

"Just having a last smoke."

"Wanted you to know I don't hold you accountable for none of this business."

"Thanks. Who'm I talkin' to?"

"Charlie."

"Good night, Charlie."

"Good night, son."

Kurt fought to quell the anger that rose up in him. Now he knew where Gunn was, sleeping away from the camp. A loner. Or an outcast. Seemed that he was under some suspicion from the drift of Curly Cow's conversation.

In the dark, Kurt smiled.

He looked forward to morning.

He already knew who his next target would be.

CHAPTER FOURTEEN

Evie Masters sweltered in the unusual heat. The night was sultry. Next to the river, the humidity was stifling. She gasped for breath, loosened the bodice of her nightgown. The girls slept deep. Their breathing added to the humidity inside the covered wagon.

Crickets chirped on the shore, and the deep boom of bullfrogs punctuated the interminable sawing sounds of the insects.

Laura turned over once in her sleep, but did not awaken. Betsy lay on her stomach, snoring lightly.

Evie sighed, sat up. It would be impossible to find the paper fan at this hour. It was buried under blankets or trunks. She loosened the drawstring at the front of the wagon, drew in a breath. It was cooler outside. She grabbed her light wrapper off a nail, pulled it behind her as she crawled outside on the seat. She had no idea what time it was. Late. The stars were bright, profuse in the night sky.

Gunn was not far away. Was that the real reason she couldn't sleep? Did this explain why she felt so hot? So restless? She had not been able to get him out of her mind ever since he had come riding back with Gordie Winesap. Gordie had calmed down after her talk with him. She made him see how wrong he was about Gunn. It had not been easy. She had pointed out to him how dangerous it had been for him to go after Gunn, try to shoot him. Most men would have just shot him dead given Gunn's advantage. Instead, the tall man with the grey eyes had merely disarmed him, brought him back to his friends. Surely, she pointed out to Gordie, that must prove that Gunn was no ordinary man, no Jonah. Then, at supper, she had watched Gunn. He sat alone, but he made it a point to be polite to everyone. Obviously, he bore no grudge. The early whispers and grumbles had changed to tones of respect. All except for Sid. He was acting as crazy as Gordie. More than once, she had caught him glaring in Gunn's direction.

Sid was a simple-minded man, quick-tempered, unforgiving. She had met such men. They either married a woman who would put up with their cruelty or they did not marry at all. Sid had not married, but she had seen some of the girls he had danced with, tried to become familiar with—their faces showed the bruises he had inflicted and they cringed whenever he came near them. Even Betsy and Laura avoided Sid. He was a hard worker, but dangerous when crossed. Two years ago he had nearly killed another skinner over a simple argument over who had dressed out more bulls on a kill.

A vagrant breeze blew from the river, blessed in its sudden coolness.

Evie started to get down, walk to the bank when a sound startled her. She shrank back against the canvas opening. In the stark light of the moon and the stars she saw two men step into view between the wagon and the river. One of them was Curly Cow Charlie.

"You my relief, Sid?"

"Yair, I am, Charlie. Everything quiet?"

"If'n you don't count the danged crickets and the bullfrogs. Ain't seed a thing 'tween here and where's Gunn's bedded down."

Evie felt a sudden chill, though the breeze had died as quickly as it had risen.

"He down at the end of the line?" There was a forced casualness in Sid's question.

"Little beyond. He's sleepin' like a babe."

"I won't bother him none. You take care, Charlie. See you in the mornin'."

"G'night, Sid," Charlie said wearily.

Evie heard him trudge away. It must be around midnight. Her heart was in her throat as Sid started walking west along the river. She didn't trust him—not after the things he'd said last night. The way he looked at Gunn. Now he was standing guard, his post taking him near where Gunn lay sleeping.

She considered waking John, if she could find him

in the dark. But what if she was wrong? John would be angry. He needed his sleep and would not appreciate her interfering for no good reason.

Gunn! She shouldn't even be thinking of him. She was a married woman. She had her life and he had his. To have any dealings with him whatsoever could be disastrous. Yet she was drawn to him. More so than ever, after last night. She opened her mouth, tried to draw in air. The heat was a smothering thing. Her breasts were drenched with perspiration. She rubbed her hand over them. Her palm came away, slick with sweat. Her whole body was clammy with moisture. There was a restlessness in her that she could not explain. That she did not want to explain. Not to herself. Not to anyone. But she knew what was wrong. She wanted something. Something that was forbidden.

She wanted Gunn.

Evie slipped her arms into the wrapper's sleeves, conscious that she was naked under her nightgown. At least, if a lantern was shined on her, she would not show flesh through the diaphanous gown. She felt a strange sensuousness as she walked away from the wagon. She had a vague idea of where Gunn had spread his bedroll. John had asked him to stay west of camp, while the Mexican wrangler camped east of the picket path, near the horses and mules.

She was glad now that the wrapper was a dark brown, not white like her gown. She pulled it tightly around her, reached into the wagon for her shoes. Fumbling through the canvas, she found them, tucked into a corner. She pulled them out, one by one, bent over to slip them on. She laced the high buttons hurriedly, drawing the strings tight before she made the bow.

She walked away from the wagon, heading west,

parallel to the path Sid had taken.

Her heart pounded in her chest. Thoughts cascaded in her mind. Thoughts of Gunn and her own strong heat. She recognized it now, out in the open, out under the naked stars, the silver dazzle of the moon. Her loins burned, dripped with a sullen urgent heat that was wet as steam from a boiling kettle. Feelings. Feelings wild as any she had ever known. Unconsciously, she touched her hair, dabbed it back with delicate fingers. Her breasts rubbed against the soft cloth of her gown, bobbing up and down as she walked, the material stroking the nipples, sending spidery tingles through the tender flesh.

She told herself she was going to warn Gunn that Sid Blanton was on patrol. But in her heart, she knew she just wanted to be near him, to sit by his side, feel his warmth. Perhaps touch him. Listen to his deep voice in the night.

Her skin tingled just thinking about him. About being so close to him, wearing such flimsy attire. She was conscious of her body for the first time in years. Lean, firm, athletic, her body made her feel aware of herself as a person, as a woman. It felt good walking alone through the close night air, lightheaded as a young girl, going to see a man in his bed. Her senses prickled in anticipation, leaped to an alert awareness that thrilled her. She could almost feel Gunn's hands on her breasts, between her legs. Could almost feel him holding her close to his bare body as her nipples rubbed against the wiry hairs on his chest.

Now she knew. For sure. She could not deny her heart any longer. She did want Gunn. For a moment, an hour, whatever he would grant her. A sudden resolve gripped her. A boldness rose up in her mind. She didn't care about the consequences. If she could have him, lie with him, feel him inside her, that

135

would be enough to carry her for the rest of her days with the man she truly loved, John Masters. John could not give her what she wanted. She had to get it for herself. Yet it was terrifying to think of herself as being unfaithful to her marriage vows.

But it was even more terrifying to think of living the rest of her life without having experienced the reality of the vision that now gripped her. Betsy had lain with Gunn. Perhaps Laura as well. She had seen the odd look in her older daughter's eyes the past three days. A smug, self-satisfied look that had never been there before.

Now it was her turn. She was not that old. She needed a man like Gunn more than either of her daughters did. She felt that she was drying up inside, withering like a flower with no water and no sun.

She needed him now, on this black sultry sodden night; needed him to give of herself, to quench the desires that had smouldered for so long in her flesh, in her heart.

She needed Gunn because she needed herself. Her Self.

"John," she whispered to herself, "please forgive me for what I'm about to do."

Sid Blanton reached the end of the picket path, marked by a small cairn of stones, and hesitated.

Who would know?

Gunn was several yards away, sleeping. He could see his bulk on the bedroll. He squatted to make sure, sighting along the land. It was Gunn all right, a dark mound on the blankets.

Damn the man! He had no business being here. Gordie had been right. Gunn was bad news. If he hadn't gotten the Simons boys riled, this run would have been sweet and profitable. Could still be, if he was out of the way. Masters was wrong. There was blame to be laid. Square on Gunn's shoulders. He had made a fool out of Wayne Simons and backed Kurt down. Kurt was the dangerous one. Just like old Claude. A pure bastard.

Masters had run a tight outfit for years. Now, with so many of the old bunch gone, a lot of greenhorns were being brought in. Things were not the same. Gee-Haw and Earl getting killed. That cut it fine as hell. Two good men gone and two yayhoos in their place.

He would make it quick and quiet.

A knife. Best way to take care of Gunn. No noise, no trace.

Sid gritted his teeth thinking about it. He'd like to skin Gunn out, hang his hide on the wall, tack it to the floor. He relished the thought. He walked on, drawing closer to where Gunn lay sleeping. He felt no fear. The old anger in him had finally made a loop. Gordie had given him the push. Gordie had been right. Gunn was a godamned Jonah.

Sid looked at the small cairn of stacked stones. He laid his rifle down next to them. Stopping, he took off his boots. He listened, put the boots down gently. The mound where Gunn slept was still there. He could not hear him snoring, but he thought he could hear him breathing through the whine-saw of insects and the bullgrump groan of frogs. Across the river, the land lay dusted by silver, vacant as a graveyard, the trees frozen in the sweatsoaked stillness.

Gunn sat on a knoll, hidden by a mesquite bush.

His bedroll, stuffed with branches, a stone, bulked below him.

He had slept a good three hours, here, when a sixth sense awakened him. The decision to make up his bed

137

to look as if he was sleeping there had come hours earlier. Too many people knew where he slept. Some might want him out of the way, if he read the looks and the grumblings right.

Now, he saw a figure in a dress stealing toward his bedroll. Below, near the river bank, he saw another figure, the picket, stalking in the same direction. Soon, the two figures would meet.

He got to his feet, crept down the slope toward the woman.

Just before he reached her, he saw the picket pull a knife, heard the whick of steel sliding out of leather.

The woman stepped back, opened her mouth to scream.

He clamped a hand over her mouth, grabbed her by the waist. Then he whispered into her ear.

"Don't make a sound!"

Evie turned, looked at his shadowed face. She shook her head. Gunn released her, his hand brushing across a full breast. Together, they watched Sid stalk close to the empty bedroll. He crouched over it, lifted his arm. He struck down, the blade collapsing the blanket. The sound of mesquite crackling resounded on the still heavy air.

Sid let out an oath, stabbed again.

Gunn shoved Evie aside, started running.

He hit Sid from behind, sending him sprawling.

"You sonofabitch!" grunted Blanton, the breath knocked out of him. He scrambled to his feet, came at Gunn in a crouch, swinging the knife back and forth in front of him.

Gunn stepped sideways, began to circle out of range.

The two men danced as Sid feinted and thrust with his knife. Once he slashed close to Gunn's belly, parting the cloth of his shirt. Gunn lashed out with a fist, caught his attacker on the side of his head. Sid stepped in, tried to ram the knife in Gunn's ribs. Gunn slammed him hard with an elbow, danced away just as the blade hissed through the air, narrowly missing him. Off-balance, Sid crashed into him, the blade facing the wrong way. Gunn fell back. Both men tumbled down the bank.

The edge was slippery.

Gunn got to his feet, tried to climb back up. His boots slipped in the muddy earth. Sid rolled to a standing position, came at Gunn with the knife held out to the side, ready to thrust.

Gunn knew he was in a tough spot.

Behind him was the river. Ahead, blocking his escape, was Sid Blanton, crouching, dangerous. Blanton had the advantage. He was high, had better footing. Gunn tried to go sideways. Sid blocked his path.

Gunn tried to go back, flank Blanton. Blanton charged. Gunn sidestepped. His boot heel slid on the mud bank. His leg went out from under him. He lost his footing, fell into the river.

The current grabbed him, threatened to pull him away from shore.

But the slip saved his life.

Blanton pitched forward as his bare feet skidded through slick mud. He landed next to Gunn with a splash.

Evie came to the top of the slope, looked down in horror at the two men battling in the water.

Gunn pounced on Blanton, trying to find the knife in the dark swirl of waters. Blanton kicked away, tried to bring the knife up into Gunn's groin. Gunn grabbed his wrist. His fingers were slick with water and mud; Blanton's wrist wet and slippery. Blanton twisted, breaking Gunn's grip. The two men fell back into the water.

The current pulled them away from the bank.

Blanton's head bobbed to the surface. Gunn was waiting. He slammed a fist into Sid's jaw, felt his knuckles crack against bone. Blanton gurgled, went under, blood spewing from his lower lip. Gunn dove, grabbed the would-be assassin's legs, dragged him deeper under the rushing water.

Sid's chest burned with fire. He struggled to rise to the surface.

Gunn climbed up Sid's body, forcing him down as he ascended. The current swirled, propelled them both back toward the bank where it eddied. Gunn's head broke the surface. He gulped in air, pushed down on Blanton's shoulders.

He held the struggling man under until he felt Blanton's muscles go slack.

The knife struck his leg with virtually no force at all, then fell from Sid's grip.

Gunn grabbed a handful of hair, pulled the drowning man toward the bank. He reached out with his other hand, grabbed a cottonwood root exposed by the water's erosion. He pulled hard, until they were both out of the eddy. He found footing, stood up in the shallows. He reached down, grabbed Blanton by the shoulders, pulled him out of the water. Stepping on to a flat spot on the bank, he heaved Sid onto the bank.

Blanton lay still.

Panting, Gunn pulled him full on the bank, lay him out flat on his belly. He put a knee into the small of the man's back, letting his weight push.

Evie came down the bank.

"Is he dead?" she gasped.

"Close to it."

He worked his knee up and down on Blanton's

back. Working him like a bellows. Water gushed from Blanton's mouth. He choked, sputtered. Gunn stood up, flipped him over.

Blanton struggled to a sitting position, went into a coughing fit. The air wheezed through his throat, into his tortured lungs. He vomited and Gunn stepped away.

"You'd better go up by my bedroll and wait for me," he whispered to Evie.

"Are you going to kill him?"

"No," Gunn husked. "But I'm going to teach him a lesson."

"I—I'll wait for you."

"Yes. You're not a part of this." It was a flat statement, but she knew he wondered.

"I didn't know he would try to kill you. I wanted to warn you."

"Roll up my blankets," he said. "Wait for me."

"Yes, Gunn," she gasped, an urgent tone in her voice. Gunn stood there, dripping wet, waiting for her to leave.

Blanton was doubled over, struggling to breathe. His throat ratted with water and vomit. His lungs made agonized wheezing sounds.

Finally, he regained his normal breathing ability, looked up at Gunn. All of the fight was out of him.

"Get up, Blanton."

Blanton stood up."

"You want me, be man enough to face me in the daytime."

"Jesus, Gunn, I made a damn fool mistake."

"You sure did," said Gunn, drawing back a fist. He unleashed it with full force. Straight at Sid's jaw. There was a crack as bone broke under the impact.

Sid started to scream, but the right was followed by a hard left to the gut. All the precious air, regained after struggle, flew out of Sid's lungs. He went down like a punctured balloon.

"Don't you ever come closer'n ten yards to me again, Blanton. If you do, I'll kill you. Savvy?"

Unable to speak, Blanton nodded.

Gunn stalked away, leaving the man to pick himself up, get back to his post if he could. He sogged up the slope, drenched to the skin. His boots squished as he walked. He stopped, emptied them of water, continued on to where he had laid out his bedroll.

Evie was waiting for him, the blankets rolled up.

"Is—sis Sid. . . ?"

"He'll live. Now, Evie, you better tell me you had a pretty good reason to come out here tonight—because if your husband doesn't know you're here we're both liable to die young."

"He doesn't know. I don't want him to know."

Gunn picked up his bedroll, took her arm.

"Let's find a place that ain't so popular," he said quietly. "And you can explain to me exactly why you came out here in the middle of the night wearing just a nightgown and a wrapper."

"Gunn," she whispered, "don't humiliate me. I feel badly enough as it is. After seeing you down there in the river, I realize how foolish I am. But I didn't want him to kill you. I cared what happened to you."

He kissed her, pulled her to him with one arm around her waist.

They walked a long way, to a place where trees grew and the river made a wide bend. It was quiet there, and Gunn spread out his blankets, stripped out of his sodden clothes. He hung them from low branches to let them dry in the hot night air.

When he came back to his bedroll, Evie, too, was naked.

CHAPTER FIFTEEN

He was startled by her beauty, the firmness of her flesh. Her hips curved gracefully; her waist was small, like a wasp's. She purred as he lay beside her, took her in his arms. He kissed her again, felt her hands slide over his wet skin, stroke him hungrily.

"I wish I could see you," she said. "I wish neither of us had to hide like this."

Gunn took a deep breath, kissed each breast in turn, lingering on the nipples with his tongue. Her flesh quivered at each new place he kissed.

She arched her back, presented her breasts to him. He cupped one, laved the nipple, the aureole. She hummed her approval. He took the other nipple, hardened it with his tongue. Her response was quick, her flesh warm.

Questions flooded Gunn's mind. There was nothing wrong with Evie. Not physically, at least. She seemed to love her husband, yet she was here, with him. She was willing, responsive. Why didn't John sleep with her? He appeared to be a man. But no man would let such a woman as Evie stray far from the marital bed. Unless . . .

It was none of his business, but he knew that Evie was taking a great risk. As if she had to grab happiness when she could, where she could. He wondered how any redblooded man could fail to partake of such a willing woman, such a fullblown lover as Evie. He kissed her neck, seized with a sudden passion. His cock was rock-hard, throbbing. She took it in her hand, squeezed it tenderly, decisively. He ran a hand over her body as if to claim her, stake her out for his own. She did the same with her finger on his manhood, tracing the swollen veins, the flap of skin that ringed the crown, the velvety-tender crown, the tiny mouth at the tip. She rubbed the hot clear fluid around the entire head.

"I want to suck you," she breathed. "May I?"

"I'd be pleasured."

She sighed, slid down his muscled frame, bent her neck, opened her mouth. She breathed on him before she took his cock into her mouth, exhaling warm breath on his crown until stabbing shoots of pleasure ripped through his loins, tingled his spine. Then she pursed her lips slightly, slid them over the mushroom-shaped head. Her saliva was warm, soaked onto the sensitive flesh. Her tongue flicked around the base of the crown. A wave of pleasure surged through his manhood. Fresh blood gushed into the veins. She caressed his testicles, began to suckle him slowly, sliding him in and out of her mouth as she bobbed her head in a coital rhythm.

She moaned, lost in a rapturous haze of pleasure. Her cheeks caved in as she applied suction, drew his organ deep into her mouth, her throat. Gunn laced fingers through her hair, massaged her scalp.

"Ummmm," she crooned, speechless with the fullness of him inside her mouth.

He fought to keep the ejaculate in his scrotum from spewing prematurely. He stroked her hair, her neck, her smooth back.

She savored him as if devouring a morsel at a banquet. Hungrily, she bobbed up and down, faster and faster until her mouth grew weary, until her lips tingled from the friction. She released him, lay trembling in his arms.

He waited until her strength returned.

"I climaxed," she said, her voice laden with wonder, "at least a dozen times."

"Good."

There was a sadness to her tone that touched him. It was plain that Evie was a neglected woman. He gripped her hip, felt the contours of her thigh.

"Every time you touch me, I get all fluttery inside."

"I want you, Evie."

"Yes. Make it last a long time."

She lay on her back, submissive. Her legs swung out wide and he tried to see her face in the darkness by the faint light of stars. Leaf shadows played over her face. Her eyes glittered like jewels. He slid onto her, eased himself between her legs. She grasped him, guided him inside her damp fissure.

"Yes, oh yes, that's what I want," she breathed. Her body shook with a sudden shudder. She bucked against him, loin smacking into loin. Her fingers gripped his shoulders as the spasms of climax rippled through her. She sobbed with joy, as he waited for the riptide to run its course.

"I want to be on top for a while," she said. "Would you mind?"

"No. Whatever gives you pleasure, Evie."

He rolled over, still inside her, lifted her above him. She looked down at him, began rising up and down on his swollen stalk, nudging him with her buttocks, moving her hips back and forth. She orgasmed again and again, rising, falling in slow measured movement. Each stroke seemed to bring her greater pleasure than the one before. She became limp, collapsed in his arms.

"Now," she said, rolling over, "take me the rest of the way."

He gave her everything he had, ramming into her

until she sobbed and screamed, her body a thrashing animal beneath him. He let out all the stops, climbed to the dizzying heights until his seed boiled over. He spurted inside her while she clutched him, tears drenching her face.

He fell on her, exhausted, happy.

"Beautiful," she breathed. "I feel wonderful."

"You are wonderful."

"You make me so."

"I'm glad. You are a lot of woman, Evie Masters."

"I feel complete."

He rolled over her sweat-slick body, lay beside her, looking up at the starry sky. Time seemed to have stopped in its tracks. He did not want her to go away. He wanted to steal her, keep her for himself. But she was another man's woman and he could not do that. Yet she had given herself to him, because of some need in her that John had not noticed or been capable of fulfilling. It was none of his business, but he was curious.

"What will you do now?" he asked, after a while.

"I must go back. Isn't that what you do when you're finished with a woman? Ride on, not looking back."

"Sometimes."

"I don't mean to sound bitter. I guess I do, though. It's not you. You didn't force me. I just wish things were different, that's all."

"You love John?"

"Yes. Very much."

"That's enough for me."

"John—he, something's gone out of him. It's not his fault. He loved me, too. We are man and wife, although he no longer shares my bed. Sometimes I'm so lonely I want to scream, to die. But I don't. Each of us has a cross to bear. I suppose this is mine."

Gunn didn't say anything. He wanted a smoke, but

this was not the time. Evie had some soul-searching to do. He didn't want to feel guilty over this. Maybe John knew. Maybe he wanted Evie to have this, as long as it wasn't rubbed in his face. He wondered if Evie had considered that. It was not his business to ask.

She got up, bent down and kissed him.

"I want to go back alone. Please. I can find the way. I don't want what we had to go any further than this."

"Sid Blanton may have seen you."

"I'll kill him if he hurts John."

There was iron in her voice. He knew she meant it.

"You won't have to," Gunn said quietly.

She kissed him again. He watched her slip into her gown, pull on her wrapper. Lace up her shoes. He didn't want her to go.

"You're a fine woman, Evie," he said. "I wish you good luck."

"Thank you, Gunn. You're very understanding. I could love you if things were different. You know that."

"Yes. I won't forget you."

"You're very kind to say that. Good night, sweet man."

And then she was gone, gliding out of sight along the moondusted plain. Gunn got up slowly, dressed, moved his bedroll again. He did not want anyone tracking Evie's path in the morning. He found a sheltered place upriver. At last, he slept.

Sid Blanton seethed with a blind anger.

Gunn had hurt him bad and he'd lost a good knife.

He had managed to walk his post until his relief came on, but he could not sleep the rest of the night. If he let Gunn get away with this, he'd be less than a man. He'd face him down. Better that, than cower

147

every time Gunn came close. Hell, he wasn't much. Lucky, maybe. He just couldn't live under that threat Gunn had made.

There was something else bothering him. Someone else had been out there. A woman, he thought. He never got a good look at her, but he had the impression it was John's wife. What was she doing out there at that hour of the night? Come to see Gunn. The thought made him even more boiling mad. Seducing John's wife. Well, if anyone said anything, he'd tell them why he killed Gunn. Maybe it had been one of the girls. Just as bad. He kenw John's feelings on that score. Did Gunn think he was better than the rest of them?

Sid got up before dawn, checked his pistol. It was a converted Remington .44. Big enough to handle Gunn, if he got the drop on him. He got out of his bedroll as the eastern sky began to pale. Gunn was out there somewhere, even though he had moved his blankets.

Sid shoved the Remington in his belt, started walking west. He'd track him as soon as it was light enough to see. Catch him by surprise this time. The bastard had been waiting for someone last night. Who? Him? The woman? Whatever, he had tricked him and that, too, rankled him.

Sid circled the camp, came up to the spot where Gunn had first laid out his blankets. He hunkered down, looking for sign as the sun turned the eastern horizon to a burnished gold.

Kurt Simons rubbed his eyes.

He had managed a little sleep. Now, his pulse quickened as he relished the thought of shooting Gunn.

He wiped the dew from the barrel of the Freund.

Rubbed the metal dry. Safely concealed, he rolled over, laid the rifle out, got into position. Across the river, he saw a man hunkered over in the spot where Gunn ought to be.

Kurt smiled, hefted the rifle. He judged the distance, set his rear sights. Two hundred yards at most. Maybe a hundred and fifty. The shadows were pulling off the land fast, the terrain lighting up as the sun climbed. He brought the barrel into line, sought his target. The front sight came to rest against the silhouette of the man.

What was he doing? Rolling up his blankets? Pulling on his boots? It was hard to see.

Not enough of him showing for a safe shot.

He wanted to be sure on this one.

Dead sure.

Kurt waited, looked back in the trees to check his horse. It was saddled, waiting, still feeding out of the bag. The reins were looped over a branch. He could get away quick; slip the bag from the horse's nose, sling it over his saddle horn; climb up, slide the Sharps back in its scabbard, jerk the reins free. He would be gone before anyone knew he had been there.

The pickets met as Kurt watched them, but did not continue their pacing. Instead, they went back to camp.

Kurt felt his nerves twang as if someone had struck a discordant string on a guitar. Soon, he knew, the whole camp would be stirring. He broke open the breech of the Sharps, loaded it. The metal parts were fancied up with wood and scroll engraving on the metal parts. He had paid a hundred dollars for the rifle up in Cheyenne at the Wyoming Armory and Provision store owned by the Freund brothers on Eddy Street.

He would need only one shot. Hit or miss, he had to

ride once he fired the big Sharps.

The man across the river stood up.

Kurt got set.

He lined up the sights on him. He could not see the man's face, but now the man's torso was in full view.

Now was the time. The man stood there, looking at the ground.

He turned his back to Kurt and Simons drew in a breath, held it. His finger arched, ready to squeeze the trigger. The sights lined up.

Kurt's finger twitched in a smooth squeeze.

The Sharps boomed.

On the other side, the man threw up his arms, pitched forward without a sound.

The shot was true.

Kurt slid back from the bank, ran, crouching for his horse. He was there in seconds. He jerked the nose bag from his horse's muzzle, slammed the straps onto the saddle horn. He mounted quickly, sheathing the big rifle, grabbed the reins. He was off as the smoke from his rifle hung in the moist morning air.

Sid Blanton studied the woman's footprints for a long time. And Gunn's. They had talked here, then moved south, apparently.

He stood up, looked around, then turned south.

A split second later, something hard slammed into his back. His breath flew from his lungs. Somewhere, far off, he heard a sound, but he couldn't tell what it was. It was just a sound as if someone had knocked once on a door. The air turned black and then he saw the ground coming up to meet him. This didn't mean anything to him either. He felt as if his lungs had been ripped out of his ribcage. He tried to draw in air, but there wasn't any. It didn't matter. Even when he hit the ground it didn't matter.

Nothing mattered anymore.

There was no air, no breath, and his insides were oozing out of him. There was no pain. He just felt as if someone was drawing a blanket over him, shutting out all the light.

And then the blanket was over him and he closed his eyes because he could no longer see anything.

Gunn heard the report, jerked up to a sitting position. He saw a puff of smoke on the opposite bank.

A man running.

The man disappeared into the trees. Later, he caught glimpses of someone riding fast to the north, but he couldn't tell who it was. He slipped on his boots, grabbed up his bedroll and started running awkwardly toward camp. He cursed himself for not having Esquire handy.

The camp was in pandemonium. Men scurried everywhere. Someone was yelling at the Mexican wrangler. The women peeked out of the covered wagon, sleepy-eyed, dough-faced. Gunn raced past them.

John Masters was asking someone to make a head count.

"Here's Gunn!" yelled Charlie Danvers. "Wasn't him!"

"See to the women!" hollered John.

"They're all right," said Gunn.

"Who ain't here?" yelled someone.

"Where'd the shot come from?"

"There's the smoke." A drover pointed across the shore. The smoke was tearing up into cobwebby fragments.

"Sid ain't here!"

"Find him!" yelled Masters.

Gunn threw down his bedroll, caught up Esquire, led him to where he had stashed his saddle.

By the time he was ready, they had found Sid Blanton.

Gunn rode by, looked at the dead man. They had turned him over. His eyes were closed. He looked as if he was asleep. Except there was a fist-sized hole in his chest. Pieces of splintered ribs jutted out of the bloody cavity.

"What the hell was Blanton doing here?" asked John. "Wasn't this where you bunked last night, Gunn?"

Gunn looked down at him.

"I moved," he said.

John's expression told him that he had many questions yet to ask, but there was no time.

"I'm going after the bushwacker," said Gunn. "We can talk it all out later."

Seconds later, he was into the river. Esquire fought the current, swam over a deep hole.

He shook off the water when he reached the bank. Gunn gave him the spurs.

He did not look back, but he felt dozens of eyes on him.

CHAPTER SIXTEEN

Gunn saw his first bull as it thundered out of a wallow, north of the Red River. The shaggy beast charged straight at him. Then a herd of over three hundred animals roared to life, scattering as Gunn rode into them. Esquire tried to rear up, startled at the awesome movement. The rider in the center of them turned so that Gunn saw his face plain.

Kurt Simons!

As Gunn watched helplessly, Simons rode with one bunch of the herd, out of rifle range. A sea of buffalo boiled in front of Gunn, turning him back. The earth shook under the mass of animals. Their hooves rumbled. A great cloud of dust rose in the air, blotting out the sun. Gunn gasped for breath, avoided a lone cow that charged blindly out of the cloud, veered away just in time to keep from bowling him over.

The herd turned as one, roaring over the plains with a sound like heavy cannons. Gunn watched them helplessly, knowing his man was safe. His tracks would be blotted out now.

Gunn sat there, rolling a smoke, waiting for Masters to catch up. He heard the thunder long after the herd was out of sight. The dust hung in the air for an even longer time, a reminder of the earthshaking power of even such a small herd. He could imagine how it must have been when thousands of buffalo roamed the plains, often stampeding so that dust lingered in the air for days. He had seen such herds up north, from a distance, and wondered how the Indians could have ridden through such a mass and not feel total fear and helplessness.

Masters rode up, as the wagons halted.

"How many head?" he asked.

"Three hundred at least."

"Good, we'll track 'em."

"I saw the man who shot Blanton, the others."

"Recognize him?"

"Kurt Simons."

Masters frowned.

"Damn," he said. "That makes it bad. We've had rivalry, but now old Claude's gone too far. Sticking his

153

eldest on me like that. He ought to pay. Hanging him would be too good."

"Be hard to prove. My word against his."

"You've got it right, Gunn. It can't be proved. But Kurt Simons will pay for those lives he took."

Gunn let out a breath.

"Seems to me you got all of them to fight if you pick any of 'em."

Masters gritted his teeth. They made a hard porcelain sound in his mouth. He jerked his reins, turned his horse.

"Come on, let's get ready to run buff. I want you to look at some rifles, pick out one to use."

The women had already started to put up jerky and hardtack. The Mexican wrangler began saddling horses. Masters didn't have to give any orders. They all knew that a herd had been jumped. The reek of buffalo was strong in the nostrils.

Masters rode to the gun wagon. Men unwrapped rifles, spread blankets on the tailgate. They laid the rifles out. Gunn and Masters dismounted, walked to the tailgate.

"That's my first buffalo rifle," said Masters, pointing to a Sharps at the end of the row. "Bought it off'n Colonel Richard Dodge. It's a .40-90-320. That stock is walnut, imported. Weighs twelve pounds."

"Fine rifle," said Gunn.

Masters touched the scope that ran full-length along the top of the barrel. "That's a one-inch tube telescope made in Jena, Germany by Vollmer. It's twenty power. Came with plain crosshairs. I added upper and lower stadia hairs calibrated to cut an elevation of thirty inches at two hunnert yards. First bull I ever got liked to scared me when I saw him through that scope. Brought him up real close. I squeezed the trigger and he dropped without a sound."

Gunn picked up the rifle, looked through the scope at a rock two hundred yards away.

"See what you mean." He set the rifle down.

"That three hunnert and twenty grain bullet was a mite light. I loaded up four hunnert and twenties and did a heap better."

Masters showed him a pair of smaller rifles.

"My reserves. That first one's a .40-70-320. Use it for deer and antelope. The other one's a .40-90-420, for elk, bear. Both of them use bottleneck cartridges. Guess you think I'm a fool for falling for that round. Hate 'em, but the rifles are fine. The cases will stick when the rifles get hot, but they'll do for back-up."

They walked down the line. Masters stopped at a big Sharps, unlike any rifle Gunn had ever seen before.

"That's my favorite," said Masters, picking up the rifle. "It's a .45-120-550. Take a look."

He handed the rifle to Gunn. It was heavy. He saw the name stamped on the barrel: Special Old Reliable.

"They call it the Buffalo Sharps. Cost me two hundred thirty-seven dollars and sixty cents. They don't make many of 'em. That scope is twenty power."

Gunn looked at the set triggers. The front trigger was used to cock the rear one. That made the rear trigger active, set it to a hairtrigger pull. A man could just touch it and it would go off.

"A beauty," said Gunn.

"I've shot buff with it at long long ranges. It's deadly up to a thousand yards."

Gunn's eyebrows lifted.

But he knew John wouldn't lie. He was serious.

"Must use a helluva load," he said.

"I load my own, for about twelve and a half cents a round. Factory loads cost two bits."

Seeing the rifles laid out, listening to Masters talk, the seriousness of these men began to dawn on Gunn. The drovers, hunters and skinners were hanging on every word, though doubtless they had heard them all before. Masters was a professional. He knew what he was doing, was careful down to the tiniest detail.

"Buy my bullets from a man in St. Joe," Masters continued. "Uses a sixteen to one allow of lead and tin."

Masters reached into an oily box, pulled out a bullet. He held it up on display for Gunn's benefit.

"Got to use a patched bullet like this. Factory loads are always paper-patched, like this one."

"You use paper too?" Gunn asked.

Everyone laughed, including Masters.

"Sure we use it when we can get it. Got a supply now, matter of fact. But when it runs out . . . paper don't grow on sagebrush out here."

"What do you do when you run out? I heard of men using thin deer hide," said Gunn.

"No good. Too thick. Antelope kidskin's O.K. Best is antelope intestine. You clean it real good and let it dry out. It works just fine."

Gunn knew he was getting an education. He was grateful. The men seemed to accept him now. Masters was making sure.

"Powder now, that's real important too," said Masters.

"You use duPont?"

"When I first started shooting buff, I used either duPont or Hazard. Good powders, well-made. Gave the balls good energy. But they burned hot and dry. Caked up the barrels. Threw off the accuracy after a few shots. Ran into a Britisher out hunting one day and tried his brand. Well, he had two, and I tried 'em both. Those were Curtis and Harvey, and Laurence and Wilkes. They were both F-gee grained, but they burned perfect. I switched to those brands on the spot, got 'em shipped to me out of St. Louis."

Masters walked to the wagon, picked up two cans of Fg powder. One was labeled Curtis & Harvey, the other was Laurence & Wilkes.

"They burn a lot wetter'n the domestic powders, develop a hell of a lot more energy. Rifles ain't so hard to clean after a shoot, neither."

Gunn was impressed.

"Seems like a slow powder to me," said Gunn. "Big grained."

Masters laughed, slapped Gunn on the back.

"You know something, I see. The Sharps needs a lot of time to build up steam. When that bullet goes out, it's traveling. The F-gee is a good powder load for those big bullets."

Masters put the canisters back in the wagon, took Gunn back to the blanket.

There were other rifles laid out, including a couple of Hawkens in .50 caliber, some long Kentuckies, percussions, and some weatherbeaten Sharps that were not fancy. Gunn picked up one of the Hawken rifles. Their day had probably passed, but the rifle he held in his hands was beautiful. A single-shot percussion muzzleloader, the rifle had seen much care. Its stock was well-oiled, with only a few nicks in it. The barrel was browned, had held up well. He put it to his shoulder, sighted through the rear buckhorn, lining up the blade front sight.

"You fancy a Hawken?" asked Curly Cow Charlie. "A fine buffalo gun if you can load fast enough. I generally carry paper loads, just bite off the end and pour the powder down the barrel, start the ball and ram 'er home. Slip a cap on that nipple there and you're in business."

"I grew up with muzzleloaders in Arkansas," said Gunn. "Put meat on the table with a Pennsylvania long gun. Downloaded for squirrel, put about sixty-five grains of double F in for deer."

Charlie grinned, looked at John.

"I think we got us a Hawken man here," he said.

"Fix him up with some powder and ball," agreed Masters. "But I'll expect you to hold up your end once we get on a herd."

Gunn's eyes glittered with pride as he hefted the Hawken once again.

"I'll do my best. I heard once that the militia, during the Revolutionary War could load and fire in under twelve seconds. That good enough?"

"Might be," said Masters, "if you can do it. If you shoot true, you can take longer'n that between shots. This British powder will keep your barrel moist and give you more shots, but you're going to have to run a patch through the barrel after every half dozen or so. Dip the patch in a little alcohol and it'll give you a quick cleaning, dry fast so you don't have wet powder."

Gordie Winesap brought Gunn a possibles bag of deerhide, loaded with powder flask, ball, percussion caps, nipple wrench, spare nipples, a wire pick, patches, a box of ball and powder wrapped in paper for fast loading. Gunn smiled, thanked him. A cheer rose up as Gunn slung the bag over his shoulder, slid the ramrod out from under the barrel, opened the patch box and screwed in a cleaning worm. He ran a patch through the barrel, examined it. A little dirt and rust marred the patch. He ran another one through and another, until it was clean and dry.

Masters nodded his approval.

"Let's ride," he said.

Rifles clattered as men picked up their weapons.

Jed loped off after his horse.

John spoke to the women, briefly, then came back to talk to Gunn privately.

"Want to show you something," he said, "before we take to the trail."

The two men walked some distance away from the others, their backs to the men who were starting to mount up or make last minute checks of equipment.

Masters opened his coat, took out a small brass case. He opened it. Inside, there were two empty Sharps cartridge cases, a .40 caliber fitted inside a .45. The buffalo hunter picked it up gingerly, held it up for Gunn to see.

"Inside these cases," he said, "there's a vial of hydrocyanic acid. If we run into Indians, this is the way I want to go out. To be captured alive would be right unpleasant."

"Just save yourself a last bullet," said Gunn, his scalp prickling.

"And what if it misfires? No, this way is quicker, surer. I can fix you up one if you like."

"No, thanks, Masters."

John laughed, returned the deadly vial back to the brass case.

"Suit yourself. But mind your hair. Now let's say goodbye to the women and get to trackin' those buff."

Reluctantly, Gunn followed Masters to the covered wagon. There, he watched as Masters kissed his wife, patted the heads of his daughters, embraced them one by one.

"You be careful, Pa," said Laura.

"Find us a good herd," Evie told him.

Betsy didn't say anything. There were tears in her eyes. Gunn looked at Evie, who gave him a sharp look. There was a silent appeal in her expression. John walked away, gruffed a goodbye as if ashamed to show his emotions. Evie followed him a short ways, then turned and looked at Gunn again. She dropped a handkerchief. A deliberate gesture that startled him.

Quickly, he walked to the handkerchief, bent over, picked it up. Instead of keeping it, he caught up with Evie, thrust it into her hand.

"You might need this," he said. "It's got a little dirt on it. Or maybe John might like to carry it with him."

Their eyes met.

A brief flash of anger appeared in her eyes, but she said nothing. Instead, she crumpled the kerchief up in her fist and stalked back to her wagon.

"Coming, Gunn?" asked Masters, turning to look at him.

"I'm right with you, Masters."

"Glad to hear it. Wouldn't want you to dally."

As they rode off, Gunn wondered how much John Masters knew. The women and the drovers, the wranglers all waved at them.

Masters never looked back.

The herd split up in three or four groups. Something or someone, had evidently passed them, south of the Canadian River. John Masters had to make a decision. The air still tasted of dust where the herd had passed. Fresh pies smoked in the sun, sending up a pungent scent that stung the nostrils. Masters and Curly Cow Charlie tried to estimate the sizes of the herds. Gunn looked for fresh horse tracks on another tack, agreeing to meet back at the starting place in an hour. The men sucked on hardtack, chewed jerky under their horses' bellies, the only shade available.

"There's a herd of about sixty head up on the Canadian," said Masters. "We'll leave a sign for the wagons, try to run those."

Charlie set up a small tower of stones, smaller ones pointing in the compass direction of the herd. The men followed Masters, strung out along a quarter mile ragged line. Gunn had come up empty, but had spotted a dust cloud in the distance, well off to the north. He could not judge whether men or buffalo had stirred up the dust.

The trackers did not stop to eat, but pressed the herd.

Late in the afternoon, Masters reined up, took his binoculars from the saddlebags. Gunn rode up beside him, Danvers following.

Masters scanned the western horizon, adjusted the focus.

"They're bedded down," he said, "about two miles from here."

Gunn was mystified. He hadn't seen a thing. He looked at Masters, a puzzled look on his face.

"Smelled 'em," he said. "We're right with the wind for a stalk."

The skinners held back as the hunters dismounted, began the slow march to where the herd was bedded down.

CHAPTER SEVENTEEN

Gunn smelled them now.

Their scent was stong, hung in the air like the smell from an open latrine. It was late afternoon and flies ragged the men lugging the big rifles, ammunition. A thousand yards from the herd, Masters motioned them into a circle. There was Charlie, Gunn, a laconic man named Spud Wilson, two loaders with rifles, Jack Leeds and Win Blevins.

Masters spoke softly.

"Gunn, you're going to get first shot since you're packin' the Hawken. Better pop your caps now, load up."

The grey-eyed man slipped a cap on the nipple of his Hawken, pointed the barrel toward the ground, pulled the trigger. He fired three to dry the oil out of the barrel. He filled the spout from the powder flask, poured eighty grains of FFg black powder down the barrel. He greased the end of the strip of pillow ticking, put it over the muzzle. He fitted an undersized .50 caliber ball, .490 in diameter, over the ticking, cut around it to make his patch. He started the ball down with a ball starter, then rammed it home with the ramrod. He did not cap the rifle. Not yet.

"All right," said Masters, pleased at the speed with which Gunn had loaded his rifle, "I'll get you to within four hundred yards if I can. There's an old bull on the edge of the bunch that's spooky as a cat in a room full of rockin' chairs. You take him out, Gunn, if you can.

"Charlie, you and I will take left and right on the herd, biggest first, like always. Wilson, you take the spookers. Any cow or bull lifts its head starts actin' suspicious, cut 'em down. Jack, you and Win stand by with loaded rifles in case one of us jams or calls you up."

The two back-up men nodded.

"Win, keep count," Masters said. He glassed the herd again. Satisfied, he continued, "If we get over twenty, you go to work."

Blevins grinned wide.

Masters looked at Gunn, saw that he needed to

explain his orders further.

"Don't want to take more'n twenty-five head today. It's late and the skinners will have all they can handle if we do that well. Tomorrow, if we can keep this herd tight and close, we'll take some more. If we can find a bigger herd, early enough, we'll go to sixty head or so. It's wasteful to kill so many."

"Wasteful?" asked Gunn.

"Not wasteful of the buff, but of the ammunition. We don't want to wear the skinners out all at once't, neither."

"Well, John," said Wilson, with a grin, "you ain't worried about lead ball since the Army began doling it out to you for free."

"They don't dole out that English powder none," retorted Masters.

It was true that Masters got a lot of free ammunition from the Army posts. No one knew if Congress approved of such appropriations, no one cared. The Army certainly didn't care. It was tacitly understood that the Army figured that the best way to conquer the fighting plains Indian was to cut out his main source of food: the buffalo. And, the Army understood that the buffalo was much more than a source of food. The Indian relied on the buffalo for a great many other needs, including a spiritual one. As one officer told Masters and some other buff runners: "There is no other way. Only when the Indian becomes dependent on us for his every need will we be able to handle him."

Win and Jack broke out the cross-sticks, handed them out to the shooters. These were well-made, sturdy, the ends sharpened so they would stick into the ground. A rifle rested where the sticks crossed, gave the shooter a steady aim. John Masters' Sharps weighed a good sixteen pounds with the scope and it was important that he not tire and always have the rifle ready for the next shot. A herd could spook at the slightest noise or movement, but generally the boom of a rifle did not scare them.

"Any questions?" asked Masters.

The men shook their heads.

"Just don't rattle those cross-sticks," he said, gesturing to move out.

Gunn, Charlie and Masters hunched low, spread out. Blevins and Leeds hung back until the hunters had gone two hundred yards then moved slow, keeping pace and distance.

From that point on, Masters used only hand sign, and that sparingly. The closer they got to the herd, the slower they moved, the lower they went. Finally, as Masters had promised, they were within four hundred yards of the herd.

Gunn looked at Masters, then downrange where the herd grazed.

He saw the big bull.

Four hundred yards. He wondered if he'd ever made a shot that far. The Hawken was not scoped and now he wished he had taken one of the Sharps.

He set up his cross-sticks. The ground was hard, but he got the points started, shoved hard to set them. He set the barrel atop the X, got to a comfortable sitting position, his knees drawn up, spread wide. He cradled the Hawken, hammered it back, set a cap on the nipple.

He sighted down the barrel. On the ride out, Masters had told him the rifle was sighted in at four hundred yards. The ball would have a three-foot drop.

"Aim above the hump, holt it, squeeze slow."

The bull had its head up, was looking straight at him. He appeared small at that distance. Too small.

164

How in hell did he measure for a three-foot drop? He wet a finger, held it up, trying to feel the wind. There was no wind. That was one thing in his favor. The slight movement of air was from the herd, so they could not smell him. That was the part of his finger that was coolest.

He sighted again. His hands started to shake. He took a deep breath, cursed.

His hands steadied.

The bull took a step toward him, but he still presented a three-quarter silhouette. Gunn drew in a breath, held it. He had never fired the rifle before, but Masters was giving him first crack.

He stopped, looked over at Masters.

Masters had his Sharps on the sticks, was peering through the scope.

Gunn started to laugh.

Hell, there was nothing to worry about now! If he missed, Masters had him covered!

He sighted again, held steady. The bull pawed the ground, dipped its massive head menacingly.

Gunn raised the barrel above the hump, tried to estimate the trajectory at a three foot drop. He squeezed the trigger. The lightness of the pull surprised him. The rifle boomed. White smoke billowed out of the barrel. He had heard the cap snap and then the stock slammed into his shoulder. He was totally blind as far as the bull went.

He looked over at Charlie.

Charlie was smiling, holding up his hand. His thumb and index finger were curled into a circle.

Gunn quickly reloaded as the smoke cleared. He could no longer see the bull. His blood raced with excitement.

Masters and Charlie were picking their shots, firing with methodical regularity. Gunn saw dark shapes slump to the ground. Except for the sound of the rifles, it was deathly quiet. He picked out another animal. He could not tell its sex. He held for the drop, fired. When the smoke cleared, he saw the hump, immobile. He reloaded. Two buff in two shots. He felt pretty good about that. The herd started to get restless. He saw cows move over to nudge the dead bulls, sniff at their shaggy carcasses. He looked at Masters.

Masters was a study in total concentration. The big Sharps bellowed; smoke and flame belched from its muzzle. A bull rose in the air, came down with a crash that shook the ground.

Gunn picked a moving target, led it slightly. The Hawken cracked, bucked in his hands. The buffalo stopped, startled by the spurt of dust two feet in front of it, a dozen yards downwind. Gunn cursed, reloaded clumsily as the pressure mounted. He was too slow. Charlie and John were outshooting him.

Masters motioned that they were to move in closer. He turned to the rifle backup men and waved them in to the position the hunters now held. Masters started crawling toward high ground some two hundred yards distant, to the northwest.

Gunn and Charlie followed, carrying their cross-sticks and rifles cradled in their arms.

The grazing herd did not seem to notice them as they crawled to the high ground two hundred yards distant. Masters waited until the other two men were set up, then took aim on a huge bull in the center of the herd. His rifle boomed. The bull fell without a struggle. Charlie shot a cow that wandered over to investigate. The cow pitched forward, fell, sending up a cloud of dust.

Gunn picked a target. A large bull wandered away from the herd, looked up at them, or seemed to.

Gunn brought him up in the scope, held on its shaggy chest. He squeezed the trigger. The bull jumped backward, then crashed over on its side.

They fired steadily into the herd before Charlie wounded a cow. She bawled and the herd began to mill. Gunn killed the cow, but the herd drifted off. He started counting downed buffalo. The barrel of his rifle was hot. He had run an alcohol-soaked patch through the barrel three times, had shot a dozen balls, missing twice. Twenty-eight buffalo lay still.

The wagons and the skinners came up. Masters signalled to them.

The herd moved off to the north. Masters brought up the binoculars, watched their progress for a long time.

The skinners went to work, Jed Randall among them. They worked until after dark. Gunn, Charlie and John Masters lay in the shade of a wagon until the sun went down, talking about the afternoon's shoot. Gunn's shoulder began to throb.

"Tomorrow, you'll shoot the Remington," said Masters to Gunn. "It's a single-shot, .44-90-400 with a Malcolm 10X telescopic sight. Plain crosswires. You did well with the Hawken, though. Ten buff in two hours. Respectable."

"Hell, that was fine shooting with a strange rifle," said Charlie. "You got eyes like an eagle, Gunn."

"I just hope the Remington has a padded stock," said Gunn.

Masters and Charlie laughed.

"They stood for us," said Masters, "and they'll stand again. They joined up with another herd."

"What?" asked Curly Cow Charlie.

"Up on the Canadian. Saw 'em plain in the binoculars."

"Why didn't you say something?" asked Danvers.

"You two were so wound up I was afraid you'd start chasin' 'em."

Gunn chuckled. He liked these two men. They were efficient, deadly riflemen. He felt easy in their company. There were not many he could say the same about.

"Sorry we didn't get a chance to let Blevins and Leeds up for a shot," said Masters, filling his pipe with tobacco. "Tomorrow, we'll let 'em shoot with us. Nobody's green any more."

Gunn knew he was talking about him. It didn't matter. Often a man had to prove himself before he was accepted into any group.

"Let's go down for the skinning," said Masters after his pipe was lit. "My stomach's growling something fierce."

They had eaten fresh tongue and seared liver earlier, after the first hides were taken, the fires lit. A snack to tide them over. Now, the air reeked of blood and the wet undersides of hides.

Gunn watched Jed and Gordie skin out a huge bull in the flickering firelight. Lanterns bloomed on the grassy plain and the banter of happy men floated on the night air.

Masters sent out scouts, trained to ride so they wouldn't spook a night herd of buff, walked among the men, slapping them on their backs, giving them words of encouragement and praise. Danvers helped two men wrestle a bull on its belly, brace the legs outward.

The bull Gunn watched being skinned out was full-grown. It was one he had shot. The animal was at least ten feet long, stood higher than a man on its feet from hoof to hump.

"What'll he weigh?" he asked Gordie.

"Close to a ton, maybe more. Big feller."

The coarse fur was a dark brown, mainly, but patches of yellow and black contrasted with the primary color.

The skinning finished, Jed and Gordie laid out the hide, fresh side up, panted at the wet weight. The cuts had been made crosswise at the nape of the neck and the length of the spine, the skin pulled off the body, laid out for the meat cuts.

Gordie cut out the boss, the hump and hump ribs, the fleece, the boudins, liver and tongue. He got on his belly and cut off the testicles.

"Vittles," he said. "Help me pack it to the kettle."

The men feasted on hump and ribs, the women joining in. Gunn saw Charlie dip a chunk of raw liver, fresh cut, into the bile and eat it raw amid much laughter. Others did the same. The boiled hump was delicious, the ribs, roasted on a spit, tasted fine, mixed with marrow and melted fat.

At the end of the meal, tongues were dug out of the hot coals, passed around to one and all. Gunn savored every chunk, though his belly was full.

The boudins, the intestines, though, tasted best of all, having been seared over the flames until they crackled with juices.

Gunn lit a smoke, lay against a wagon wheel. If they were attacked, just then, he knew he would be unable to move. A bottle of *aguardiente* was passed around, and he sipped at it, a perfect capper to a perfect day.

Moments later, the scouts came in, young Chris Mills and a teamster called Angel Face, whose pocked features, broken nose and toothless grin, made him a standout.

"We got company," said Angel Face. "Other side of the Canadian. Spotted their fires."

"See who it was ?" asked Masters.

"The Simons," said Chris. "I snuck up on 'em. They got the herd spotted too. Must be more'n two hundred head in it now."

"Good," said Masters. "We'll be set up on our shooting sticks before dawn. You boys come eat now. You done good. Real good."

Gunn looked at Masters, then at Evie.

Her face was drawn, flickered white in the firelight. She put her hand on her husband's arm.

"Do you have to go against Simons?" she asked.

Gunn held his breath.

"It's our herd," he said stubbornly. "And it's on this side of the Canadian. Simons has got no claim on it."

"But, we can go on, up to the Cimarron."

"No!" Masters barked. "And damn Simons if he gets in my way!"

CHAPTER EIGHTEEN

Gunn felt strong hands on his shoulders. He came awake, reached out, grabbed the man shaking him.

"Easy, son, it's Danvers," said a whispered voice. "Time to run some buff."

Gunn shook off sleep, sat up. He had seldom slept so soundly. He looked around, but saw only a dark shape where Charlie's voice sounded. It was dark as pine pitch, even the stars were blotted out. In the air, he could smell rain.

He joined the others after saddling Esquire. Leeds, Blevins, Masters, and Danvers waited for him. Masters handed him the big Remington, two boxes of ammunition.

"Try this, Gunn," he said. "I'd like to get twenty-five buff down before the sun gets high."

They moved out well before dawn, following Masters' lead.

He seemed to have an instinct for finding the herd, even in the dark. An hour's riding brought the five men close enough to smell the heady musk from the herd and the dank scent of the river.

Masters held up, tapped each man's leg as a signal to dismount. They put nose-bags on the horses to keep them quiet, walked the rest of the way on foot. In the darkness, Gunn heard the grunts of the buffalo, the faint snorts and chuckles of animals drinking at the river's bank.

"If they cross the river," Masters whispered, "we'll have to swim or wade across. Keep your powder dry."

Dawn hovered just over the horizon as the five men fanned out, stalked the herd from downwind. Gunn used bushes and a gully for cover as he stole across the land. The sounds of the buff were louder now. He judged the herd to be large from the sound of them. Water splashed, and the earth shook as buffalo jumped in and out of the water. He figured they had fed most of the night and were logy and slow.

Coming over a rise, he was conscious of a mass of animals milling below him. He stopped, holding his breath. He would never find a better spot. He sat down, found a soft spot and drove in the cross-stick stakes. From the noise of the herd, he gathered it was spread out all along the river. He had no idea where the other men were. It was spooky, lying there in the darkness, waiting for dawn to break.

He slipped a shell into the chamber of the Remington, working the action slow. Any odd noise, such as metal scraping, could spook the buffalo he knew. It was a mistake he had no intention of making. He laid out his shells by feel, memorized where they were.

Slowly, the sky lightened in the east.

The herd loomed up out of the darkness so close he

171

thought they must surely see him. But he was hidden behind a mesquite bush that appeared magically in the dawn light. Buffalo were everywhere he looked, stomping their hooves, snorting, playfully ramming one another, jostling for positions at the great drinking fountain of the Canadian River. As the light broadened, he saw animals all up and down the bank, some belly deep in the water. Their massive horned heads were a beautiful sight to behold. He felt the first tremblings of buck fever, looked for signs of the other men to quell the fluttering in his stomach, calm the shaking of his hands.

Charlie was two hundred yards to his right. He saw Blevins fifty yards off to his left. He wet a finger, tested the air. Still downwind. The slight morning breeze blew off the river, cooled his finger, washed over his unshaven face. He could not see Leeds nor Masters.

But, moments later, he heard the Sharps buffalo gun boom. He saw a bull drop far downstream. White smoke blew back from Masters' position. Gunn picked out a bull, set his shoulder dead in the crosswires and fired. The bull jerked as the 400-grain lead bullet hammered into its heart. He ran twenty yards, stopped. Blood streamed from its mouth. Its tongue protruded, its eyes rolled, bloodshot with pain. Gunn opened the breech, slammed another shell in the chamber. The bull swayed there on braced legs, its eyes glazing over with death. It swayed from side to side, stamping impatiently at the earth, pawing it in a final dull anger.

Gunn watched the huge beast with a mixture of sorrow and self-loathing. Finally, the bull raised its matted head and bellowed. His hooves slipped and he tried to pull them back, but his strength was gone. He rolled to one side, hit the ground with a thud. The bull twisted its head and seemed to look straight at Gunn with accusing eyes. Purple blood spurted from its mouth and nostrils. It went into a convulsion, its body shaking with a last spasm of life. With a last, sobbing gasp, the bull stiffened and its head fell with a crash. The mountain of flesh and hide lay accusingly in the dirt, quiet as a stone.

Angrily, Gunn picked another target, a huge cow staring at the dead bull. He fired, saw it stagger under the impact as its lungs burst. He could not look at this one die, but quickly reloaded the single-shot rifle.

He lost count of how many shots he fired, but the herd was so spread out that there was no stampede during the twenty minutes or so that he brought down more than a half dozen animals. A bull raced off at full speed right past him and he thought he must have missed. But its bloody roar sounded fifty yards past him as it lost power, its legs crumpling under its massive weight. The bull skidded a dozen feet, dead as a doornail from a lung shot.

The barrel was so hot, he stopped shooting.

That's when he realized that others were firing too—from across the river. He saw them through the haze of dust and smoke. Kurt Simons, Wayne, and men he did not know. Beyond them, the skinners waited by the hide wagons like statues in buckskin.

Part of the herd started across the river. The Simons bunch shot them in their flight until the water roiled with blood. Chunks of the herd scattered, finally realizing their numbers were being decimated. Some turned away from the river, swept upstream on thundering hooves. Blevins had dropped four or five bulls, took a cow on the run. Charlie shot a bull point blank in the head, saw the bullet spang dust from the rugged head and then had to run as the animal charged him, horns lowered for the kill. The air reeked of blood and burnt powder, of sweat and the musk of buffalo.

The herd scattered and the firing died down.

From across the river, came the sound of angry shouting.

A large man stood up. Gunn gathered it was Claude Simons.

'Masters! This is our herd! We had it staked!"

Masters strode into view, his pipe smoking, his rifle laid across his cradling arm.

"Claude, we run this herd here yesterday."

"You sonofabitch!"

Gunn reloaded, stood up, his rifle at the ready. He saw, out of the corner of his eye, that Danvers had done the same. Blevins stood up a few minutes later. It was a standoff.

"You get the buff you shot, these on this side are ours!" shouted Masters.

"Goddamn you, Masters, ours is all in the fucking river!"

"Then skin 'em out, Simons!"

Skinners with ropes started wading into the river downstream.

Gunn turned and saw their own skinners swarming up on foot. The wagons rumbled to a halt fifty yards away in plain view of the Simons bunch. Jed took the bull Gunn had dropped behind him and started skinning it. It was already on its belly and Jed was on his own. Masters walked along the river counting the dead animals.

Skinners swarmed over the nearest dead ones.

Masters came up to Gunn, casual as a man out for a morning stroll. The sun was not yet high but the flies boiled over the carcasses of the buffalo.

"You keep a sharp eye, Gunn. I counted forty-two buff on this side."

"Some of 'em may have been downed by the Simons bunch."

"A few. But this is my herd."

"Why not take what we know we shot, leave the rest for them?"

"What're you sayin'?"

"Share this herd with them, move on. Give Simons the buff on the banks."

"Never!" Masters' face turned beet-red.

"Then we better get set for a donnybrook," said

Gunn. "We're liable to be skinning out some men before this day is over."

"We'll take all the buff this side of the Canadian," said the implacable Masters, turning on his heel.

Gunn cursed, knowing there would be trouble because of John's stubbornness.

Simons ordered his men to tie ribbons on the horns of the buff he had killed. They worked the bank and they hauled the bulls across on long ropes with mules pulling hard. Masters watched their every move. The skinners traded sharp insults back and forth, and tension built between the two groups of hunters eyeing each other warily as the skinning went on.

Gunn helped lug hides to the wagons to help speed things up. Masters and Danvers continued to patrol, their rifles loaded, to keep Simons honest. Gunn couldn't help noticing that Kurt Simons sat on the bank, unarmed, as if to ensure against someone shooting him. He looked at Gunn often, knowing Gunn would not shoot an unarmed man. He had proved that in San Antonio during the face-off with Wayne Simons.

Then, someone shouted.

"Big herd coming!"

"Buff!" yelled Blevins.

The skinners scattered. Men from Simons' bunch sogged out of the river, went for rifles. There was yelling, confusion, as a herd thundered toward them, raising a huge cloud of dust in the air.

Evie, Laura and Betsy ran to the covered wagon, got inside.

Gunn mounted Esquire. Masters and Charlie got on their mounts too.

"Injuns!" Jack Leeds raced past Gunn.

"Get the wagons moving!" yelled Masters. "Keep 'em tight!"

Wagons rumbled as drovers cracked their whips.

The herd was a long way off, but Gunn saw bronzed

figures on horseback racing beside the animals. Puffs of smoke were followed, seconds later, by the sound of the rifle reports. Buffalo fell from the herd, skidded dead on the plain.

"Comanches!" hollered Charlie Danvers.

"We'll have a fight of it!" Win Blevins wheeled his horse, streaking past Gunn toward the onrushing herd.

"Try for the lead bull!" ordered Masters as Gunn kicked Esquire hard in the flanks. The big sorrel galloped after the others.

The herd split as Masters dropped a charging bull. Some of the Comanches followed the herd that split off to the south. The main body of the herd followed the river, a mass of shaggy bodies shaking the earth with the thunder of hooves.

Dust billowed into the air, choking and blinding the hunters.

Gunn tracked a buffalo with the Remington, lead it four feet, fired. The cow bellowed as the bullet ripped into its lungs. It staggered on, blood gushing from its mouth and nostrils. He reloaded, wrapped the reins around the saddle horn, letting Esquire have his head as he tried to guide the animal with his knees. He heard the whoop of the Comanches now.

Across the river, Simons led his hunters into the water. Some fired from mid-stream, dropping buff down the sloping banks. Noise and confusion, mixed with the blinding dust enclosed each man in a small violent world of hurtling buffalo, gunsmoke and blood.

Gunn saw Jack Leeds go down as a bunch of buffalo crashed into his horse. The animal screamed in pain. Then, all was blotted out as dozens of buffalo overran the downed horse. He tracked the leader, shot it dead in its tracks. Reloaded the smoking rifle and raced along with a bunch of buffalo at breakneck speed. The ground was laced with holes, burrows and ditches that threatened to break Esquire's legs, send him hurtling out of the saddle. A giant buffalo emerged out of the dust cloud and charged him. Gunn grabbed for the reins, turned Esquire just in time. He chased the buffalo, exhilarated by the excitement, the danger. He caught up to it, aimed, fired pointblank into the animal's spine. The great beast raised his matted head, glaring white-eyed before its legs collapsed. The animal fell, and Esquire leaped over it. Gunn hung on, his teeth rattling.

A mass of buffalo loomed out of the throat-clogging dust. Gunn lost all sense of direction. A Comanche warrior, clad only in breechclout, raised his rifle, aimed at Gunn. Gunn swung his rifle, fired from the hip. The Indian's head made a sickening sound as it bounced along the hard ground.

Esquire stumbled as it tripped in a depression, recovered. Gunn dropped three bullets before he got one in the chamber. Now he felt as if he was in the middle of the herd. Animals passed so close to him he could feel their hot breaths on his trousers. He shot until his gunbarrel was hot and still they came. Their noise was deafening. His eardrums throbbed with the sound of their endless hooves.

Now and then he heard a shout or a Comanche scream.

But he saw only buffalo.

The rifle weighed a ton in his arms. He lost the strength to raise it to his shoulders and began firing with the barrel rested on the pommel. He dropped two cows and a bull before he rode into a clear patch on high ground, the dust motes sparkling in the sun, a patch of blue overhead. Around him streamed the buffalo, racing into the dust, their tongues leaking out of their mouths, their eyes bulging with fear.

John Masters stayed with the leaders. Unknown to Gunn, he and Charlie managed to keep the herd turned, milling in a huge circle. The Comanches, in the rear, kept the herd moving. It was a field day for men on horseback, with plenty of shooting and danger to keep their blood racing.

A wagon splintered as buff overran it. One of the drovers screamed, went down. He was trampled into a bloody mush, his flesh torn to shreds by the knifing slash of hundreds of hooves.

Evie broke out of the dustcloud in the covered wagon, pulled to a stop in a grove of cottonwoods. The other wagons formed a protective circle. She and the girls stood up to look at the dust cloud, watch the action. Lone buffalo streaked past, were dropped by excited drovers with barking rifles. An Indian rode by, looked at them curiously, wheeled, rode back into the dust cloud with a wild whoop.

It was a strange, unreal scene.

Gunfire from unseen rifles sounded above the roar of the galloping buffalo. Buffalo dropped from shots that came from an unknown direction, a ghostly hand, an invisible shooter.

Gunn was driven from his position by a mass of buffalo, charing Comanches.

He saw one of the Indians go down, tumbling eerily into the path of two large bulls who ground his face to a pulp as they trampled over him one by one. A man appeared on horseback, Wayne Simons. He looked at Gunn, then disappeared in a sudden rising of dust.

The sounds of the hooves began to diminish.

Gunn dropped a bull and a cow in quick succession as his vision improved.

Riding through the lingering dust toward the river, he shot two more stragglers, saw Charlie Danvers, his face emblazoned with dust, ride out of a smoky gully, grinning.

"We got into 'em, didn't we, son?"

"For sure," said Gunn.

"Let's find John, see if he's all right."

"Something wrong?"

Danvers scowled.

"Saw him being chased by three howling Comanch'."

No more'n ten minutes ago."

"Let's go!"

The two men rode out onto the plain. Now they could glimpse dead buffalo, other men riding back out of the dust cloud. Humped bodies lay where they had fallen. They shot two wounded animals, but there was no sign of John Masters.

Claude Simons appeared out of nowhere, stopped when he saw the two men. He was chewing on a chunk of raw liver, his mouth smeared with blood.

"You boys lookin' for Masters?"

Charlie nodded.

"Last saw him he was hightailin' it east along the river, a bunch of Comanch' doggin' him."

"You didn't help him?"

Simons threw back his head and laughed.

"We got skinnin' to do, Danvers. You boys won't be doin' much. We're claimin' this herd."

Charlie's face hardened to stone.

"I ought to shoot you right out of the saddle. Claude. You never was no damned good."

Claude laughed again.

Kurt and Lucky materialized out of the dust, stopped next to their father, fingering their rifles.

"You better get your bunch together and go after your boss," said Claude, his face wiped clean of any smile.

Gunn looked at Kurt, lay his rifle crossways over his pommel. Kurt's mouth slipped into a smirk.

"Too bad you boys had to go to all this trouble for nothin'," he said. "We're stakin' out this herd."

Gunn spoke for the first time.

"You got some accounting to do for three good men," he told Kurt.

"Now?"

"We'll get Masters loose first, take our share of this herd," said Gunn.

"Mighty big talk for a man wha't outnumbered."

179

Kurt nodded. Gunn turned, saw Wayne Masters on his flank.

It was a tough situation. He wanted to blow Kurt out of the saddle, wipe the smirk off his face. Wayne's rifle was leveled at him, casually lying across his horse's neck.

"Let's get out of here," whispered Charlie.

"You boys better move," said Claude. "My skinners'll be all over this ground in a minute. They got orders to shoot anyone tries to put a knife to any of these buff."

"You sonofabitch," husked Danvers.

"Let it drop," said Gunn.

He rode past Wayne. The dust rose in the air, thinned. In the distance he heard the whoops of the Comanche. His blood turned cold.

Charlie followed him out of earshot of the Simons family.

"Didn't think you was one to back down, Gunn," he said. "I'm mighty disappointed. We could have got two of 'em at least."

"Maybe. I think Wayne had me cold. That other one Lefty?"

"Yair."

"Well, he had you to the wall. A pistol out of sight in his left hand. We'd not have done much."

"I don't know."

"I figure our time will come. Let's go get some help, find Masters."

They rode toward the wagons at a gallop. A pair of Comanches rode by in the distance, silent as ghosts. Gunn didn't like it. He didn't like it at all.

CHAPTER NINETEEN

The skinners were moving the wagons, ready to move in when Gunn and Danvers rode up to the cottonwood grove.

"You men hold up," said Gunn.

"Who're you to give orders?" asked one man he didn't know.

"Masters is in trouble. Simons gave the word to his bunch to shot any of you skinners who go out there."

Evie came up, curious.

"What's this about my husband?"

"Comanch' a-chasin' him," said Charlie. "Mighty sorry, ma'am."

"I need a couple of men," said Gunn. "Jed, Gordie. Want to come?"

Both men nodded eagerly.

"I'm coming too," said Evie.

"Better not," said Gunn.

She glared at him, hiked her skirt.

"I'm coming," she said defiantly. "Pablo, saddle my horse!"

Pablo ran to the supply wagon, lifted a saddle onto his shoulder.

Jed and Gordie were right on his heels.

Gunn looked at Evie Masters, saw the fear in her eyes. He knew that John's chances were not good. The last two Comanches he had seen were riding in for the kill. John was outnumbered, probably low on ammunition. He thought of the cyanide capsule inside the Sharps cases. He might have to bite the bullet unless they could get to him in time. He didn't like the idea of Evie going along, but he sensed that she knew the situation as well as anyone. It was probably something they had talked about before. Maybe more than once. Something in Evie's eyes told him that she knew the seriousness of the situation. She went back to the wagon and he did not see her until Pablo brought up her horse. The skinners grumbled, stood in a bunch, watching Simons and his crew attacking the dead buffalo with skinning knives.

"Don't even think about it," Gunn told them. "You'll be shot in your tracks if you go out there. Wait until we get back."

"Hell, you know Masters ain't got a chance," said Angel Face.

"Shut up," said Charlie, as Evie got out of the wagon. She wore pants, a man's shirt. She had a .45 Colt strapped on her hip.

"I heard," she said. "I'm ready when you are, Gunn."

"You keep up if you can," he said. "I'm not going to go slow."

"I'll keep up."

Laura and Betsy pleaded with their mother not to go. She shook them off, took the reins from Pablo.

"Stop her!" Laura said to Gunn. "Please!"

Betsy hung back, glowering.

Gunn shrugged.

"Let her go if she wants," said Betsy. "She doesn't care about us."

"I'm thinking of your father!" said Evie, climbing into the saddle.

"He's not my father!" blurted Betsy.

Evie dismounted quickly, strode to her daughter and slapped her hard across her face.

"You shut your ungrateful mouth!" she said. "How dare you say such a thing!"

Betsy cried.

Gunn and the others watched in stunned amazement as Evie whirled and remounted.

"Come on," she said. "The longer we stay here, the less John's chances are."

Gunn shook off his bewilderment, spurred Esquire. He wiped dust off his mouth, spat as his horse caught up with Evie.

"What was that all about?"

"None of your business," she said tightly.

They rode in the direction of the Comanche yells, getting stronger as they galloped toward a small dust cloud in the distance.

John Masters pulled his pistol, fired at the Comanche

charging up behind him. He twisted in the saddle, pulled the trigger. The pistol went off in the Indian's face. Smoke blotted it from view, but the warrior twitched, fell away as his horse galloped on, riderless.

Behind him, blood-chilling shouts curdled his flesh.

He heard a rifle boom in the distance. His horse faltered. Another rifle cracked close by and his horse wrenched him as it stumbled again. He heard the thudding whack of the bullet rifling into muscle and bone. The sky careened dizzily as the earth tilted. John hung onto the saddle horn as the horse went down.

He hit the ground hard, felt a shattering pain in his leg. Heard the sound of bone crunching. His vision went black for a moment. The horse twitched, tried to rise up. Masters jerked his leg free. Excruciating pain shot through his hip. He pulled the rifle free of the scabbard, laid the Sharps across the horse's rump. The horse was dead. Masters' leg was broken, crushed from ankle to kneecap.

He laid out his ammunition, checked his pistol. He had five shots in it, another half dozen in his belt. He counted the Sharps cartridges. Ten.

The Comanches approached warily. There were seven of them. They fired a couple of shots. Bullets thunked into the dead horse. Tufts of hair flew from the wounds. John, fighting down the pain, drew a bead on a Comanche. He got him in the scope, squeezed the trigger. The Sharps barked, slammed into his shoulder. The Indian fell without a sound. A wild war-whoop bellowed from a dozen throats. The Indians fired at him, blistering the air with buzzing lead balls.

Two more Indians rode up, shouting, gesturing.

Now there were eight Comanches out there, in range of the buffalo gun.

One started to circle, come up behind him.

John tracked him with the Sharps, shot him out of the saddle. The others charged. John switched to the pistol, emptied it. He drove them back, reloaded the pistol with shaking hands. He had only three rounds now that were in the revolver's cylinder. He loaded the Sharps, waited.

Beads of sweat popped out of the pores on John's forehead.

Shoots of pain coursed through his broken leg, bored into his brain. He fought down the nausea, the queasy sickness in his gut. Sweat dripped from his brows into his eyes, stinging, blinding. He wiped the moisture away, stared dizzily at the Comanches boldly riding back and forth shouting obscenities in their language. One of them dismounted, lifted up his loincloth, insulting him with the strongest gesture he knew. He displayed his genitals as he strutted toward the wounded man.

Joh held his fire.

Another bunch of Comanches rode up.

He counted nine of them. They talked, and eight rode off, back up the river.

The man who had given the Comanche insult remounted his horse, charged straight at Masters. He hung low on his horse, under its belly. John tried to get him in the crosshairs of the scope. He rose up slightly, to fire. He couldn't see the Indian clearly, but he shifted his aim to the horse's chest. He saw a puff of smoke, felt a stinging slap in his arm, followed by a horrible pain that numbed his senses. His left arm throbbed. He forced himself to fire at the horse. He squeezed the trigger. The horse dropped, the Indian hit the ground running.

Charged, jerking a blade from inside his loin cloth.

Blood gushed from John's arm.

He picked up the pistol, shot the Indian ten feet away. The ball caught the warrior in the chest. He skidded, off-balance, on his heels, lay in a twisted heap.

The other braves screamed their anger, began to circle.

A spool of dust rose in the air.

Masters fired at one Indian without aiming. The Indian kept circling.

Masters looked off to the right where two warriors came at a gallop. He heard a shot from his left. A bullet whined over his head, raising the hackles on his neck.

He swung the rifle and two more shots sounded on his right. One of the balls caught him in his hip. He heard the bone shatter, felt a searing pain. Blood soaked his broken leg, shattered hip.

John shot the pistol until it was empty. The range was too great. He fumbled for the Sharps cartridges. His fingers were doughy, useless things. The loss of blood began to make him lightheaded. He felt, amid the excruciating pain, a feeling of lassitude, of euphoria. He wrestled with the big Sharps, could barely lift it. He could no longer use the scope. The land blurred in it. He could find no target.

Realizing that he was outnumbered, almost out of ammunition, John reached into his coat, grasped the brass case holding the cyanide capsule. Images floated in and out of his mind, meaningless.

He opened the brass case, took out the empty Sharps cartridges. He pulled them apart, looked dully at the cyanide capsule.

There was shouting and shooting, but it all seemed so far away.

Gunn started shooting his pistol as he rode down a Comanche. The Indian flew from the wooden saddle, hit the ground stone dead.

Charlie and the others fired, too. The Comanches scattered.

Evie came riding up, shouting her husband's name. They saw John lift something to his mouth.

"No, John! No! We're here!"

Gunn shot a Comanche riding hard up behind

185

Masters. The Indian tumbled out of the saddle. He looked at Masters, saw him put something in his mouth. He cursed, suddenly sick to his stomach.

The Comanches rode off. Gunn and Evie dismounted, raced toward Masters.

"Spit it out, John!" shouted Gunn.

As they drew close, Masters crunched down on the capsule.

The deadly cyanide worked instantly. Fumes rose up in John's nose. He looked at them with dull glazed eyes and twitched once before he fell over, dead.

Evie, hysterical, rushed to her husband, slapped his face, trying desperately to bring him back to life.

Gunn stood watching, then looked up to see the running fight the Comanches put up as Charlie, Jed, and Gordie harried them west up the river. Rifles cracked, men yelled. The sounds faded. A silence deepened around Evie and her dead husband.

She crooned to him, unmindful of Gunn standing there, a buckskinned figure holding a rifle, throwing his shadow over her as she rocked her husband's head in her arms.

"John, I'm sorry. I never meant to hurt you. Not with Betsy. It just happened. I'm sorry she found out. But she loves you. Yes, John. She loves you like a true daughter. I didn't mean to do that to you. So long ago. I didn't know my mind then. I didn't know what was happening. You don't know. I didn't want you to know. If I had told you maybe none of this would have happened. You would have killed him. Maybe you would have gone to prison. I won't tell Betsy—ever. Nor Laura. God, I'm so sorry, John."

The smell of bitter almonds wafted to her nostrils. John's mouth was open, bits of paper-thin glass glistening on his teeth. She began to weep. Her sobbing wrenched at Gunn's heart. He put a hand on her shoulder.

"Let him go," he said quietly.

He offered her his hand. She turned, looked up at him. His face was in shadow, his head lit by the morning sun behind him. She took his hand, lay John's head down tenderly on the ground. She saw his leg bent, winced. A deep sob caught in her throat.

Gunn pulled her to her feet.

"I'm sorry," he said.

She wiped fingers across her face, under her eyes.

"He was a good strong man."

Then she fell into Gunn's arms, wrapped her arms round his waist, held him tightly to her. But she no longer wept.

"Come," he said, "there are some things yet to do. I'll send a wagon for John."

He led her away. She turned once, looked at her dead husband, then looked away quickly.

"I want his rifle and pistol," she whispered to herself. "I'll dress him out fancy, bury them with him. Here, where he died, by the river. We—we'll mark his—his place with a stone."

"Wasn't Betsy his daughter?"

"No. She found out. The night she was with you, I think. I think that's why she went with you. She told me about it. I don't blame her. She was angry, hurt. I tried to keep it from her. Wayne Simons told her. I hate him for that. You made him look foolish. He struck back the only way he knew how."

Gunn was puzzled. She stopped, looked at him frankly.

"I never told this to a soul. I'm telling you. Why, I don't know. Years ago, when John was gone, a young, handsome man came by wanting to join John on his hunts. Laura was four years old. I was miserable. I took him in, thinking John would be back soon. He didn't come and I—I lost my head. I slept with this man and Betsy was born. Oh, I know she is this man's daughter. John did not come back for nearly three months and I was already showing by then. I told John

187

about it and he—he didn't hire the man. Maybe things would have turned out better if he had."

"Who was the man?" Gunn asked, already knowing the answer. Even as he spoke, he suspected, and then a sudden shot of insight burst into his mind with perfect clarity. A hunch, a glimpse of a man who looked so much like Betsy he wondered why he hadn't seen it before.

"Claude Simons," she said simply. "He was the man, a drummer then, with a foolish dream of hunting buffalo with the best there was."

Claude Simons saw them coming. Eight Comanches swooping down on his skinners. He rallied his sons, shot it out. A few more Indians rode up, whooping war shouts, followed by Curly Cow Charlie and two other men. The Comanches struggled to escape the crossfire. One of his skinners screamed, a lead ball pounding into his shoulder.

The firelight lasted only a few moments. An eternity.

Gunn and the skinners rolled the wagons in on the heels of the battle.

Buffalo lay scattered for miles along the river, out on the plain.

A silence settled on the battlefield, the acres of dormant buffalo stiffening in the sun. The clouds had long since dispersed and there would be no rain. The hide wagons rumbled to a stop. Evie and her daughters pulled their wagon up, set the brake.

Claude stood there, defiant, hard as a statue. Kurt, Lefty, and Wayne stood a few yards behind him, their faces frozen into masks.

"Evie," said Claude. "Did John make it?"

"No," she said. "He bit the bullet."

"Like he always said. A fine good man. I wish . . . but you better get your men out of here. We lay claim to this herd."

"I'm a widow now, Claude. I know that this is our herd. Some of it anyway. We'll share or we'll fight, but you won't drive us off."

"You were a widow a long time ago, woman," he said angrily. "Don't push me now."

Gunn rode up, Jed flanking him. Curly Cow Charlie sat his horse a few yards away. Gordie eased his horse closer, sensing something important was about to happen.

"Kurt," said Gunn. "I'm calling you out. For murder. Three men."

"Gunn," said Claude, "hold up or I'll spill you on the ground."

The Remington lay crosswise on Gunn's saddle, but he held it there with his left hand. His right hand hung near his pistol holster.

Skinners gathered, from both sides, sensing the danger. They stood in groups, facing each other. Kurt Simons handed his rifle to Lefty. He braced himself for a pistol draw. Wayne lay his rifle down, spread his legs, waiting, also, to draw.

No one moved for a long time.

Jed looked at Gunn, sensed the odds.

"Gunn," he said, "don't push them. Not now."

"Yes, now," said Gunn. "Claude, step out of the way. I have no quarrel with you."

"You do," said Claude.

"No!" Evie exclaimed. "No! Stop this!"

Claude was slick.

Gunn had to hand it to him. He was smooth as a pair of ladies' silk stockings. He brought up his rifle with one hand, his finger inside the trigger guard. It was only a slight movement like a man shifting his weight from one foot to the other.

Gunn's hand flew like a diving shadow to the butt of his Colt. The pistol cleared leather so fast no one saw it. Not Claude, not Kurt nor his brothers. Not Jed nor Evie nor her two daughters. No one saw it and the thumbing back on the hammer was part of the swift movement. The pistol bucked in Gunn's hand and Claude staggered backwards into Lefty's arms, a dark purple hole in his chest right where his heart pulsed. Ribs disintegrated, the heart exploded into bloody pulp. A fist-sized hole in his back sprayed Lefty with blood and minute shavings of bone.

Kurt drew, his hand flashing fast toward the butt of his pistol.

Time stood still, like a rope at the end of a throw before it falls.

Gunn's pistol moved slightly, the barrel snout focusing on Kurt's chest. Orange flame and white smoke blossomed at the explosion. Kurt caught the ball in his breastbone. A look of stark surprise lit his face. He sucked at breath, choked on blood.

Lefty saged under the weight of his dead father.

Wayne got his pistol clear of the holster, brought it up with a shaking hand to aim at Gunn. Instants froze. Moments hung like drops of oil in a vacuum. An eternity crossed slowly as he saw he wasn't going to make it. Gunn was already down on him, the Colt .45 staring into his eyes, deadly as a snake.

Gunn touched the trigger with a firm squeeze.

The Colt spoke, deadly as lightning from a black thundercloud.

A black dot appeared above Wayne Simons' eyebrows, dead center in his forehead.

"Jesus Christ," said Jed Randall. A murmur went through the crowd.

The Simons bunch backed off. Smoke curled from the barrel of Gunn's pistol.

"I've got three shots left," he lied. "Lefty?"

Lefty half-sat, his father's body sagging in his arms.

"You win," he said. "We'll bury our dead, move on out."

"You take what you killed, no more," said Gunn.

"John Masters would have done the same."

"The hell he would've," said Lefty. "But we'll take your offer." He broke down, then, began to sob.

Gunn dismounted. Evie, too. She came to him.

"You," she said, "would you consider . . ."

"No. No I wouldn't. Evie, you've got to pick up the pieces of your life, go on." He looked at the dead buffalo, the skinners already at work. He saw the dead animals as the end of something. A Comanche lay still in the sun, his hair shining like a crow's wing, feathers making a sound like a quill pen point scratching across blank paper.

Betsy walked over to Claude, looked at him, then at her mother. Then, she ran, her arms outstretched, into Evie's waiting arms. The two women hugged each other a long time.

Laura came over to Gunn, spoke quietly.

"I—I don't understand. What's wrong? Why did Betsy do that? You know, don't you?"

Gunn took her hand.

"Take care of your mother. Be good to Betsy. And remember that people are weak inside at first. It's only life makes 'em strong."

She gave him a peculiar look.

"Claude Simons. He resembles . . ."

"A lot of people. Don't ride so far you can't get back easy."

"Gunn . . . you're some kind of man, you know. But you're not staying, are you?"

"No. After we get the hides to Dodge, I'll be moving on."

"You could stay. Mother, she—she likes you. She . . ."

"It wouldn't work and you know it, Laura. I love you all. You, Betsy, Evie. I'll think of you. Might even see you again.

He squeezed Laura's hand, walked back to his horse.

191

Esquire stamped a forefoot on the ground. The sound was strangely empty, but Gunn thought that he could hear far away, the awesome sound of buffalo shaking the land with their thundering hooves, barreling up to the Cimarron like an earthquake rolling over the earth under a cloud of dust shimmering like signal-smoke in the late afternon sun.

He holstered his pistol, climbed up into the saddle.

His ears throbbed with the distant sound of buff . . . running, running across the plains forever like a black cloud of hooves and horns carrying a shaggy black mass toward some green valley far beyond the bark and whump of killing guns, far beyond the clapboard towns and railheads, the range of the Sharps rifles and the long telescopes.

Betsy looked up at him. Her eyes flashed, but there was no hatred there.

He had killed her father. Her real father.

He sensed that she wanted to tell him about that. Wanted to say something to him.

But she didn't say it.

And life was hard as stone sometimes, but man wasn't a stone and he could bleed. Claude Simons and John Masters were dead, their blood soaking the ground.

Maybe, Gunn thought, the buffalo was dead too. As game, as hide, as food, as life for the Indian.

Death was sad, that's all.

Damned sad.